Private Duty C.N.A.

-By Sherre Still

Contents

Working Hard

Another day working with these bitches ordering us Patient Care Technicians around like little kids, Maxine thought as she gave a fake smile to one of her co-workers. She rushed to get on the packed elevator not wanting to wait for another one and risk clocking in late. She quickly made a space for herself and rode with the crowd to the ninth floor.
By the time Maxine made it to the time clock, there was already a single-file line of employees clocking in for work. *Shit, something told me to get out of bed ten minutes earlier than usual,* she thought glancing at her watch. It was 7:01 a.m. already. Standing last in line, she ended up clocking in ten minutes late.

If I do not get a chance to eat my lunch before two o'clock today, I'm calling off work tomorrow. I don't care how short staffed they'll be, she thought wearing her fakest smile into the break room.

"Good morning, everyone," she said as she opened her locker.

Only a few of her co-workers responded.

Well, it looks like my day is going to be a real shitty one. Most of these so-called professionals will not even speak but are going to care for patients who look just like me with a smile plastered on their faces. Ain't that a bitch?

After putting her things away, Maxine sat at the table with her co-workers to get a report on the patients she would be caring for that day. The charge nurse assigned her to work with Peggy, a registered nurse she was not too fond of. Word traveled fast among co-workers, so everybody knew who worked well with others. Let's just say Peggy wasn't one of the good ones to work with.

Peggy had recently graduated from nursing school and was looking to "get lucky" in marrying the first doctor that saw her G-string through her thin white uniform pants. She made it her business to show her cleavage when the doctors made their rounds, displaying her double-D breast implants.

After receiving her patient list, Maxine went straight to the laundry cart to get linen for her patients. *There is nothing like waiting for hours for the laundry cart to be re-filled and not having your patient beds made and baths done* Maxine thought as she got all of what she needed. Maxine then went for her usual cup of coffee for an energy boost. Out of nowhere, Peggy came walking down the hallway swinging her blonde hair extensions over one shoulder.

"Maxine, can you help Mr. Dotson in Room 9105 with his shower before the transporters come get him for surgery? And our patient in Room 9111 wants some cereal without milk and a container of orange juice please," Peggy said with a fake smile.

This bitch didn't even speak this morning. Now she's up in my face with a smile asking for me to do this and that, Maxine thought. She walked over to the nurse's station to give Peggy a dose of her own medicine with a smile right back.

"Hey Peggy, the keyword is 'our' patient. I'm going to get a cup of coffee before I get started for the day. Mr. St. Charles in 9110 is bedridden and needs the most assistance, so he will be the first person that I tend to. You are well-equipped to take care of Mr. Dotson needs. I'll be right back," Maxine said before walking away to get a cup of coffee.

Peggy couldn't believe that Maxine had the audacity to express herself as she did in front of the other nurses. Peggy was a bitter person, because it took her nine years to complete a four-year degree and become a registered nurse. She got a thrill out of belittling others to make herself feel good.

Once Maxine returned to the floor with her cappuccino in hand, Ms. Hyson, her supervisor, called her to the office. Trying not to take offense when being called to the office, Maxine sat quietly until her supervisor spoke.

"Maxine, did you refuse to assist Mr. Dotson as Peggy asked you to do?"

Maxine's response was sincere. "Ms. Hyson, I wouldn't say that I refused to do anything. I have six patients and out of all of them

Mr. Dotson can do for himself. Mr. Dotson is NPO because of today's surgery so he can't eat anything."

Maxine continued her defense, "Peggy must not have been paying attention when receiving report by the night nurse, as there is an NPO sign over Mr. Dotson's bed. Since Mr. Dotson doesn't have an IV in his arm, I asked Peggy to make his bed while he showered before going to surgery. I didn't feel like there was anything wrong with asking Peggy to do so since Mr. Dotson is our patient."

Ms. Hyson decided to question Maxine about the most important duty of her job as a Patient Care Technician. "Are the vitals for all of your patients entered in the computer?"

"My vitals were keyed in the computer before I left the floor, Ms. Hyson," Maxine replied, feeling a little irritated that her boss was now picking on her.

Ms. Hyson checked the computer and saw that Maxine had entered all the vitals for the patients she was taking care of. Leaning back in her office chair, Ms. Hyson didn't feel the need to waste any more of Maxine's time. Maxine gladly left her supervisor's office, laughing on the inside about Peggy's attempt to get her in trouble.

On her way out, Maxine saw J.T., one of the other techs that Maxine enjoyed working with. He rubbed his goatee as he walked toward her to deliver some good news. "What's up Maxine?" he asked, wiping sweat from his forehead.

"Hey J.T., you better keep walking because boss lady will be coming out of her office shortly, and we can't afford to be getting a write up if we ever plan to transfer to another department. You know what we're trying to do. Right?"

"*Fa sho, fa sho*, Maxine. We need to make *mo'* money and do less work. The beds are made, and baths are done for your patients in Room 9104 A and 9102 A and B."

Maxine gave J.T. a friendly smile after learning she didn't have to complete those tasks for her assigned patients.

"Thanks J.T.! I owe you one big time."

"Well don't just thank me, Maxine. Peggy helped with the patient in Room 9104, while trying to seduce me and get me to do something I shouldn't be doing on the job. I had to ignore her advances. A *brutha* like me needs his J.O.B," J.T. said in a serious tone.

Just then, Maxine's pager started vibrating, letting her know that she and Peggy were receiving another patient just admitted to the floor.

"Thanks again J.T. for helping me out. When you get ready to go to lunch, find me so that I can give you my badge. You can charge your meal on my card," Maxine said before walking away.

J.T. waved his hand, refusing the lunch offer as he proceeded down the hallway to drop the dirty laundry down the chute.

As the hours passed Maxine worked nonstop: drawing blood on patients; doing EKGs; and collecting stool and urine samples to send to the lab as the doctors requested. Feeling a bit overwhelmed, she couldn't believe she was receiving another patient. She gathered a wash basin, toothbrush, comb, sample size tube of toothpaste, body wash, lotion, and mouth wash.

Before long, it was lunch time so Maxine texted Peggy letting her know that she wasn't working another 12-hour shift without eating lunch like she had done the day before. Maxine texted Peggy from the secretary's desk for a second time before preparing to leave the floor to eat lunch. **Hey Peggy, I'm going to lunch,** the message read. Maxine let a few minutes pass while she waited for a reply from Peggy. When Maxine didn't receive a reply from Peggy, she proceeded to leave the floor.

Maxine pushed the break room door open and instantly got upset. She saw Peggy along with all the other nurses laughing and talking about random stuff while eating lunch. Maxine was thinking about how hard she had been working all day, feeling her arm pits sticking to her shirt.

"Peggy, those are some nice pictures of you at your parents' lake house in Florida," a nurse said while eating lunch with Peggy.

Maxine worked hard to keep her composure as she grabbed her wallet from her locker and left the break room without saying a word. *I must find another job. It's time for a change,* she thought as she waited for the elevator. Her vibrating pager broke her train of thought. **Your patient has arrived on the floor :),** the message read. *Shit,* Maxine thought as she walked to the patient's room to introduce herself. The elderly woman was relaxing in bed trying to fall asleep.

"Hi, my name is Maxine. I'll be your Patient Care Technician for the day. Peggy will be your nurse. She'll be in shortly. Is there anything I can get you after I take your vitals ma'am?" Maxine asked with a friendly smile.

"No, there's nothing that I need right now. I just need some rest. I've been sitting in the emergency room all morning long. If you hadn't said anything about not being my nurse dressed in that white uniform, I was going to ask for some pain medication to relieve this headache I have," the patient said as she sat down on the bed.

Peggy walked into the patient's room when the patient made the comment, making it perfectly clear that she was the registered nurse.

"Ms. Pete, I'm your nurse Peggy and this is your aide Maxine who will take your vital signs while I do your assessment and gather your personal information. Did you bring any medication from home with you?" Peggy asked, trying to be professional.

Ah the title to my occupation is Patient Care Technician since you want to be technical about it bitch, Maxine thought as she stood there in the room looking at Peggy talk to the patient. Maxine couldn't help the fact that she was well put together in her uniform and the patient thought she was the nurse.

"Peggy, I'm going to lunch now that you're back working with our patients. Ms. Pete's vitals are taken, and I will enter them in the computer out in the hallway," Maxine said as she was about to leave the room.

"Thanks for informing me that you were about to leave, but you can't go to lunch just yet. Our patient is back from surgery, and you will need to get vital signs on him every fifteen minutes for the first hour and then once every hour after that," Peggy said with a fake smile as she had presented earlier that morning to her co-workers. Maxine just gave Peggy a blank stare because she didn't want the patient in the room to hear what she really wanted to say. Peggy knew she had finally gotten under Maxine's skin by her facial expressions shown.

Dr. Slone, one of the cardiac doctors on the floor, walked toward Maxine as she walked out of the patient's room. He greeted her with a friendly smile. Standing six-foot-six weighing two hundred sixty pounds, Dr. Slone had a brown skin complexion with sandy brown hair. He wasn't bad to look at, indeed he was a handsome man.

"Hello Maxine, how is your day going?" Dr. Slone asked as he smiled at her.

"My day is going ok, Dr. Slone. I'm just counting down the time until I clock out and go home. I didn't get a chance to eat lunch or rest my aching feet, so I'm looking forward to going home," she said as she applied lotion to her hands.

"From what I can see, the Cardiac floor has been busy. I read a few of the charts on my patients, and the secretary said you all have been receiving patients back-to-back," he responded glaring at the transporter bring another new patient.

Secretly, Dr. Slone wondered what it would be like to be involved with a person of Maxine's nationality. She was intriguing.

"I know you haven't had lunch, Maxine. I have no problem going to get you a sandwich and something to drink," Dr. Slone said still smiling at her.

"No thanks, Dr. Slone. I have a patient that just got a pacemaker and I need to complete taking the vitals, so I'll talk to you later," she said as she waved and walked away. Dr. Slone watched as Maxine switched her hips hurriedly from side to side rushing to her patient.

Heading Home

It was 7:34 p.m. Maxine should have clocked out 34 minutes ago to go home, but she was still working – assisting a patient with a bed pan and changing linens soaked by another bedridden patient she had been caring for throughout the day. By the time Maxine got ready to go home, Peggy had left for the day and the evening crew was getting ready to start their shift. Intuition made Maxine go back to check on Mr. Dotson, the patient that received the pacemaker, because she knew the last hour vitals were not done. She put her belongings back in her locker and walked to Mr. Dotson's room. After she charted the vitals, Maxine rushed to clock out before anyone else could ask for assistance.

As Maxine drove home, she smiled at the thought of Dr. Slone asking if he could get her anything to eat for lunch. She had a feeling that Dr. Slone had the "hots" for her; but then wondered how many other female employees throughout the hospital Dr. Slone "cared for" when it came to lunch. When Maxine pulled up in front of her apartment and got out of her car, she ignored the neighbor's boyfriend who flirted every time he was alone.

"What's up Maxine? I feel like I'm in desperate need of some medical attention" the neighbor's boyfriend said as he looked her way.

Maxine looked in the opposite direction as the neighbor's boyfriend continued to talk while she walked to her apartment door. One thing Maxine didn't want in her life was drama from her next-door neighbor over a man that didn't respect her. *I wonder how that asshole even knows my name,* Maxine thought as she locked her front door. Relieved to be in her comfort zone, Maxine walked down the narrow hallway to the kitchen smelling burnt bologna. She was greeted by her son's friends with a smile as they spoke.

"Hey, Ms. Gamble! How are you doing?" Zachary asked as he admired Maxine's natural beauty.

"I'll be fine young man once you pick up that trash by your foot and put it in the trash can. Do you leave trash on the floor at home?" Maxine asked as she pointed at the candy wrapper.

"No ma'am, Ms. Gamble. I don't leave trash on the floor at home. My mother is a neat freak," Zachary replied as he picked the candy wrapper up and put it in the trash can.

Maxine shook her head and smiled walking out of the kitchen as she told her sons to make sure they clean up. Once Maxine was out of sight, the boys began talking.

"Dude, Myron, y'all momma is as fine as my gal is *playa*. She got that soda bottle shape body going on and shit. *Ya* feel me?" Raymond said as he grabbed his crotch.

"Nigga let your nuts go when speaking about my momma!" Myron said as he stopped eating his bologna sandwich to look at Raymond.

"Man, Myron stop getting mad at *yo* boy for giving *yo* momma compliments my nigga. *Shid*……………. Ms. Gamble is finer than a *mutha,*" Jaleel said sipping his can of soda.

Ahmad, Myron, and Chance all looked at one another thinking that their friends were out of their minds to even think of their mother as a sex goddess.

Meanwhile, Maxine had taken a shower and put on a pair of pajamas. She had brushed her teeth refusing to eat dinner because she was worn out from working hard for her money that day. She looked at her reflection in the mirror to talk to herself.

Before walking out of the bathroom to go to bed, Maxine whispered to herself, "You are a good mother. I love you. You are doing the best that you can to provide for your family."

Since the day she left her parents' home, this was something that Maxine told herself daily to feed her self-worth and to keep her spirits up. Maxine's father swore that she couldn't and wouldn't make it as a single parent with three small children and no college education.

He was wrong. Maxine was now a 29-year-old woman still holding it down on her own as a single parent raising her kids. She was raising them well, mind you.

As she let her thoughts relax, Maxine's eyelids closed peacefully into deep sleep.

15 Years Earlier

On a hot Sunday morning sitting on the first row in church beside her mother, Maxine looked over her shoulder at Oliver, the boy who caught her eye. She patted the puffy ponytail sitting on top of her head and smiled. Oliver smiled back at Maxine, thinking it was kind of funny that he was distracting her from her father's sermon. Phylencia looked over at her youngest daughter with a smile that was priceless. That smile quickly turned into a frown when she saw her daughter eyeing a "knucklehead" boy. Phylencia slapped Maxine's thigh, leaving her handprint on her leg.

"Turn your head around and listen to the word, child," Phylencia said, giving Maxine an evil eye. Maxine turned around so that she wouldn't get hit again. As soon as church was over, Maxine saw that her parents were distracted so she waved her hand for Oliver to come her way. Oliver wondered how far he could get with Maxine since she kept coming after him every time she saw him at church.

"What's up Maxine? You know you need to stop trying to get my attention. I don't want Pastor and the First Lady after me for messing with their baby girl," Oliver said. He was really just trying get some feedback about Maxine's feelings for him.

Maxine didn't care to hear Oliver's good boy speech. "Boy, please! Pastor and the First Lady are too busy with church business to be thinking about me. Why don't you come over Wednesday night around 7:30 or 8:00 so we can chill out and watch a movie or something? My parents will be at Bible Study, so there will be no need to worry," Maxine said, looking Oliver dead in the eye.

Oliver stood there for a moment to think about the offer. He liked the way Maxine kept licking her lips and smiling at him as she spoke, but he really couldn't decide if he wanted to take the chance and mess around with the pastor's daughter.

"Maxine, that don't sound like a good idea. Listen, I'm getting ready to go. I'll talk to you some other time," he said about to walk away.

Oliver turned to go catch up with a young lady he was interested in. Maxine grabbed Oliver's hand before he could walk away from her, showing how aggressive she could be.

"Stop being so paranoid, boy. Like I said, Pastor and the First Lady got other things to do. They ain't thinking about me. Do you have a car?" she asked as she kissed at him.

"Yeah, you know I have a car. Why would you ask me that?" Oliver asked, jerking his hand away. He didn't want anyone to start any rumors about them. "Well, come pick me up on Wednesday night at 7:30. The coast should be clear. You can take me someplace nice, or we can hang out at your house. Don't have me waiting on you, boy. If you do, I'm going to be mad at you," she said before walking away to give Oliver a good look at her from behind. Oliver stared at Maxine as she walked away, thinking that he would take his chances and see what the pastor's "baby girl" was all about.

Maxine couldn't wait for Wednesday to arrive so that she could be in the company of her boy crush. On Tuesday night, Maxine's cousin Tina came over to help her with a history assignment but ended up hearing all about Oliver. Tina was a year older than Maxine. She was well-built and wore color in her hair, which made her look even older than she was. Tina had the look Maxine wanted.

"Tina, when I get through with this last question on this pre-test, I want you to give me a relaxer," Maxine said as she finished writing down the answer.

Maxine wanted a new look for her first date. Tina knew how religious and strict Maxine's parents were. Nothing good came to mind when she thought about how Maxine's parents would react.

"Maxine, I don't want to get in trouble. If Pastor and your mother find out I put any chemicals in your hair, they will tell my momma and I'll be put on punishment," Tina said in a serious tone.

Maxine hated to be told no, so she lied and told Tina that her parents would approve. After Tina put the chemicals in Maxine's hair, she looked like a different person.

"You look so grown up now that your natural hair has been straightened out. You better not tell anyone I gave you a relaxer, Maxine, or I'm not talking to you for a long time," Tina said, warning Maxine. Tina felt like she had done something wrong.

Mission accomplished! I can't wait to be alone with Mr. Church Boy Oliver Boyd. He ain't going to know what to do with all this, Maxine thought as she hugged Tina goodbye. Before skipping to her bedroom, Maxine paused in the foyer grinning from ear-to-ear and admired her long hair in the mirror.

Bible Study

Pretending she was menstruating, Maxine rolled some toilet tissue together, placed it in the center of her panties and dropped ketchup on the tissue to get out of going to bible study.

"Momma come here please. I need you," Maxine called out from the bathroom as she sat on the toilet.

Phylencia was waiting for Maxine by the front door so they could head off for bible study and not be late. The last thing Phylencia wanted to do was upset Pastor and embarrass him by being late. When Phylencia heard Maxine screaming like she was dying, she threw her bible and purse down on the couch and rushed to see what was wrong.

"What's wrong with you Maxine? Why are you screaming?" she asked, huffing and puffing.

Maxine was holding her stomach while still sitting on the toilet and pretending to be in severe pain. "Momma, my period came on, and I'm hurting so bad that I can hardly stand up. Can I stay home please and get some rest?" Maxine asked sounding like she was about to cry. Phylencia saw the red spot in the center of Maxine's panties, so she let her stay at home.

As soon as Maxine heard the front door close and the lock click, she hopped off the toilet to change into something cute to wear on her date. She curled her hair and put on a little lipstick. She figured Oliver would appreciate her good looks. After she finished getting ready, she sat on the couch and waited patiently. After waiting for more than 30 minutes, she figured Oliver wasn't coming. She took off her sister's wedge heel sandals and tossed them aside. Then the doorbell rang. Maxine damn near broke her neck to get to the door, hoping it was Oliver coming to finally pick her up. Before Maxine opened the front door, she counted to 10 and rubbed her hair to make sure it was in place. She opened the door and found Oliver Boyd standing there. He was 5'8" and had a devilish grin that spread across his face. "You finally came Oliver,"

"What's up Maxine? You ready to go?"

Oliver didn't want to waste any time or risk getting caught at the Pastor and First Lady's house – not to mention, picking up their "baby girl".

"Ah yeah, I am ready to go. I thought you weren't coming to pick me up Mr. Slow Poke," Maxine said with an attitude.

Oliver made a U-turn and headed back toward the car. He didn't want to take time arguing with Maxine on the porch.

"Wait a minute. Please don't leave me, Oliver. Here I come," Maxine said disappointed that her church member was going to leave.

She ran back to the couch to put her shoes on, snatched the house keys off the coffee table and ran out of the house without locking the door. It was a quiet ride. Oliver just focused on the road and wondered what they would do next. Maxine sat comfortable in the passenger seat imagining how Oliver would passionately kiss her.

"We're here. Watch your step when you get out of the car," Oliver said as he held the passenger door open. He didn't want Maxine to fall on the gravel in the driveway.

Maxine wasn't impressed with the home. She was scared to even walk up to the front door of the condemned-looking shack. Once they walked inside, Oliver turned on the light in the living room. Maxine saw roaches crawling everywhere. *I can't even imagine drinking a glass of water in this place,* Maxine thought as she stood near the front door not wanting to take another step.

"Can we go someplace else?" Maxine asked, trying not to frown.

Oliver didn't know what Maxine's problem was. He was used to living in a house infested with bugs.

"I can take you back home, but I'm not sticking around. Or I can park my car in the garage, and we can chill out there for a minute before I take you back home," he suggested.

Maxine went along with Oliver's plan B to park his car in the garage for a while, because she didn't want to go back home. As she walked back to Oliver's car, she felt like something was crawling on her skin. Trying to seem like he wasn't bothered by Maxine wanting to leave, Oliver parked his car in the garage. He didn't have much to say it seemed. They both just sat like two ducks floating on water, doing nothing.

 "So, what do you want to do?" Maxine asked as she stared at the garage brick wall.

"What did you ask me to pick you up for Maxine?"

Oliver figured he would question her before going forward with what he wanted to do. Maxine leaned over and kissed Oliver's chapped lips. She allowed Oliver hands to roam around her upper body.

"You know I'm a virgin, right? Are you Oliver?"

"Yeah I'm a virgin too," Oliver lied. "I've just been waiting on the right person to get with."

Maxine had on a black mini skirt and white tube top, so Oliver had easy access to her body. He reclined the car seat back so that he had plenty of room to spread Maxine's legs.

"Wait Oliver; wouldn't it be better if I took my top off?" Maxine asked, willing to let him lick and suck her small breasts.

"You can take your top off if you want," Oliver said trying not to sound too eager.

He was ready for some physical action. Maxine was all hot and bothered when Oliver got in between her legs, but the more intense things got the less excited she got about having sex. Oliver, on the other hand, knew that he was getting close to smashing Maxine's private part as he fingered her clitoris. *Yeah, she's ready. That pussy is nice and wet,* Oliver thought as he continued to finger Maxine and listen to her make low moaning sounds.

"Let's climb in the backseat so that you can be more comfortable," Oliver suggested.

Maxine really didn't want to climb in the backseat, but she didn't want to be labeled as a little girl either if the word got out that she was with Oliver alone. Maxine settled on her back in the backseat, and Oliver got in between her legs as though he was about to pray. He slid her panties down and parted her thick bushy pubic hair with his two fingers. Maxine was stiff as a board and scared. She felt strange.

"You're trying not to moan, Maxine. It's okay to enjoy the feeling, baby," he said.

As Oliver continued to move her body with the touch of his hand, she moaned. Oliver eased Maxine's tube top down and licked and sucked her breasts.

"Why do your breasts taste like butter Maxine?"

"I put butter on my skin because my breasts are growing, and it hurts. Do my breasts stink or something?"

Oliver didn't answer. He went back to sucking and licking Maxine's breast. Oliver was just trying to move on to the next level.

"You're sucking too hard, Oliver," Maxine said as she tried to push his head away from her.

Oliver softened his approach as he eased two fingers inside of her.

"Damn baby, you're so warm inside," he said as he pulled his two fingers out of her to lick Maxine's cum off them.

The church girl was introduced to the freak in Oliver. She had never witnessed or heard of anything Oliver was doing to her. Inch by inch, Oliver eased his penis inside of Maxine. Maxine couldn't believe she was having sex with Oliver Boyd.

"You like that, Maxine?" Oliver asked as he began to stroke her.

Maxine didn't say a word. She just laid there stiff as a board while Oliver handled his business.

It Seemed Like a Dream

Months went by, and neither of them said a word
about that night in the garage. Maxine avoided Oliver
at church because she feared someone would put
two and two together.

One day as Maxine walked home from school in the
110-degree heat, she felt faint. She showered and
went to bed as soon as she got home, because she
figured she just needed some rest. After her nap,
Maxine spent the evening vomiting and struggling
with diarrhea. Her mom took Maxine to the hospital
just to make sure her daughter wasn't coming down
with a virus. At the hospital, Phylencia found out that
her child was four months pregnant. She sat in the
waiting room filled with disappointment as she
wondered how she would deliver the bad news to
her husband.

A pregnant teenager who was barely in high school
whose father held a position as a well-known
preacher of the largest church in the Saint Louis area
was going to be the talk of the town. All Phylencia
could imagine was her church members saying she
was a bad mother.

The house wasn't a home once Pastor found out
about Maxine's pregnancy. Pastor went through
everything in Maxine's bedroom to find a love letter

or picture of the mysterious person that got his youngest daughter pregnant. Maxine was smart enough not to have anything in her bedroom connecting her to Oliver, because she knew her daddy would kill him. There was a calendar that was marked with a red heart on the day Maxine first had sex, indicating that it was a planned activity. Pastor showed the calendar to his wife and argued that she should have kept a closer eye on Maxine. Phylencia and her husband tried to use threats to get Maxine to out the father of her child, but she wouldn't give up Oliver's name so easily.

The first chance Maxine got to be alone with Oliver, she skipped school to tell him the news. *Man, I should have used a condom. Maybe if I ask Maxine if she is sure I'm the one who got her pregnant she'll get mad and leave me alone. Naw, that would be a lame-ass cop out. I'll just deal with it,* Oliver thought as he grabbed Maxine's hand.

"It's cool that you are carrying my baby. I'm going to take care of mine," he said.

Oliver wasn't sure how he was going to help raise a baby, but he was willing to accept his responsibility. Maxine thought she would be with Oliver forever after he assured her that he was going to be a father to their unborn child. As the baby grew inside of Maxine's body, she didn't feel or look the same. Maxine looked in the mirror every morning to see how many more stretch marks had surfaced overnight on her breasts and stomach.

Things began to get more and more complicated for Maxine. She couldn't eat whatever she wanted, because she feared she would throw up or gain too much weight. Then Oliver had been missing in action because he was hiding from Maxine's parents. He feared she would tell them he was the father.

One day at lunch, fried foods were served, so Maxine called her mother and asked her to bring a salad to school. One of her classmates overheard the conversation, and word of Maxine's pregnancy spread fast. By the time Phylencia arrived with Maxine's salad, her classmates were whispering about her. The principal called Phylencia to come get her daughter from school after a teacher told her about Maxine's pregnancy. The principal recommended that Maxine transfer to Continue Education, a school for pregnant girls. Many changes came her way over those next few years of high school.

By the age of 17, Maxine was the mother of three and had graduated early from high school with honors. She was offered many college scholarships but decided to stay at home with her parents to raise her children and work full-time. The journey wasn't easy for Maxine. She dropped her children off at daycare every day and worked as a Patient Care Technician at Mercy hospital.

Maxine figured once her children got older, she would go to college and get a degree. She was determined to be successful and prove her parents wrong. Once Maxine saved up enough money, she moved out on her own and never looked back – no matter how tough times got for her and her children.

Maxine was a notable example for her children. She worked every day of the week, only taking one weekend off a month to spend quality time with her boys. She wanted to teach her sons that nothing in life was free, and that hard work pays off sooner or later. Maxine thought about how good God was to have brought her through so many situations that no man could have helped her out of.

"The car note, electric and gas bill are the only bills that need to be paid since I doubled up on the rent two weeks ago. I should have some extra money to get my hair done if my calculations are right," Maxine whispered to herself before falling into a deep sleep.

Another Day

Even though Maxine didn't get to take her lunchbreak the day before, she decided to go to work anyway. After working for about three hours, Maxine was glad that she went to work. The day was going well, because she was working with a nurse that didn't mind getting her hands dirty.

"Maxine, you can go ahead to lunch. I can handle the last few patients who need help with their beds and baths," Tiff said as she entered information about a patient in the computer.

"Thank you so much, Tiff. You are a pleasure to work with. I wish we worked together all the time."

"I know what it's like to be a Patient Care Technician. That's why I have no problem lending a helping hand if I can. Nurses should be required to make at least two beds and help with baths during their shifts, but you and I know that's wishful thinking," Tiff said finishing the patient's bed.

"You are so correct. You should bring that topic up at our next staff meeting. Would you like for me to bring you something back from the cafeteria?"

"No thanks. I brought my lunch from home.

I'm on a budget because I'm trying to save money to buy a house. Go on ahead and enjoy your lunch break."

As Maxine exited the elevator, she spoke to a few of her co-workers from another floor as they entered the cafeteria. The aroma of the food made it hard to decide what to eat.

"I'll have a grill chicken sandwich on sourdough bread with cheddar cheese."

"Can you make that two and add French fries with them both," someone said standing behind Maxine.

She quickly turned around to see Dr. Slone smiling at her. "So, I take it today is a good day since you're here in the cafeteria ordering lunch."

"Yes, Dr. Slone, it's a great day. I don't feel like my job is in jeopardy today since I'm not working with my boss' best friend," Maxine replied with a friendly smile.

Dr. Slone put their food on his tray, got them something to drink and paid for their lunch. Maxine wondered what Dr. Slone's conversation was going to be about over lunch. They settled down at the table, and Dr. Slone took a sip from his drink.

"So, Maxine, I can see that you're not married. Are you dating someone?"

"No, I'm not dating at the present time, Dr. Slone, and really don't have time to date. I work a lot."

"So, I take it you don't have any children since you don't date and work a lot?"

Maxine was caught off guard, *"Dr. Slone is a bit out of line with the personal questions…with his nosey ass."*

"Excuse me, Dr. Slone, but I don't believe my personal business is any of yours," she said, trying not to be offended.

"I didn't mean to offend you, Maxine. I was just trying to have general conversation that's all. What I really wanted to ask is if you would go out on a date with me? I was a bit nervous and maybe said something stupid. I'm not trying to offend you," he gazed at her as he finished his sentence.

 "I don't think that would be a good idea, Dr. Slone."

Maxine kept eating her lunch like the question didn't bother her. Just then, her pager started vibrating.

"Dr. Slone, thanks for lunch. Next time it's my treat. Ok?" she said getting up from the table.

Dr. Slone nodded his head in agreement and watched Maxine walk away.

There's Always Something Going On

Maxine returned to the Cardiac floor to help with a few patients that were being admitted and discharged. After she got everything settled, she was surprised when the charge nurse allowed her to leave work three hours early. Maxine felt blessed to be getting off early on such a beautiful day.

Since it was a good day, Maxine figured she could do something fun with the boys. *I'm going to pick the boys up from school so we can eat dinner together and watch a movie,* Maxine thought as she drove to her sons' school. Maxine pulled up just minutes before the bell rang. Ahmad and Myron were walking out of the school building behind a group of girls when they heard their mother calling their names. The boys ran toward their mother's car, happy about not having to ride the bus home.

"What's up, Momma? Is everything alright?" Ahmad asked hugging his mother from the back seat of the car.

"Hey Ahmad, don't hug me so tight. You both are acting like this is the first time I've ever picked you all up from school. There's Chance coming out of the school building. Catch that big-headed boy before he gets on the school bus," Maxine said as she smiled at her sons.

Myron hopped out of the car to get his brother. They walked back with their arms around each other's shoulders and rapped to the beat they were making. "What's up mommy moms? Is everything good?" Chance asked.

"Everything is fine. I just wanted to pick my handsome sons up from school if y'all don't mind," Maxine said laughing.

The boys didn't respond to their mother's comment. They were too busy yelling goodbye to their friends out of the car window. As Maxine stopped at a red light, she glanced at her sons and was glad she never took the easy way out and had an abortion.

As soon as they got home, Maxine showered and started dinner. It didn't take long for her to cut up, wash and fry the chicken she had thawing out since that morning. The boys did their homework until dinner was ready.

"As soon as the macaroni is done, you all can eat dinner," Maxine said after sweeping and mopping the kitchen floor.

Maxine was about to pour herself a glass of wine and watch television when the telephone rang. It was the school principal calling to request a meeting with Maxine about an incident involving her sons.

"Ms. Gamble, I wanted the boys held today in the main office until I was able to call you to pick them up, but they left before the secretary could call their home room. I can schedule a meeting with you for tomorrow, but the boys cannot return to school until we meet," the principal said.

"Mrs. Turner, would you mind holding on for a second?"

"Sure," the principal replied in a friendly tone.

Maxine put the phone down and went to confront her sons.

"Did anything out of the ordinary happen at school today?" she asked with a stern look on her face and a hand on her hip.

The boys all shook their heads no and said, "nothing out of the ordinary happened at school today". Maxine wrapped up the call with the principal and decided to meet with her that evening.

The boys rode in silence as they listened to their mother use profanity while driving back to their school. Myron, Ahmad and Chance prayed that there was some mix up when it came to the principal's call. They hadn't done anything wrong in their minds.

Maxine was enraged. She had been through too much to get her boys into private school for them to act a "damn fool" and think she wouldn't find out about it.

"If something actually happened at school today, I promise you I'm going to put my hands on you all in the worst way," Maxine threatened. In a single-file line Ahmad, Chance and Myron walked in the school building behind their mother, scared as hell knowing Maxine meant business about kicking their butts when they did wrong.

Sit Down Meeting

Maxine sat in the principal's office with Mrs. Turner and Mr. Cramer, the school counselor, who joined them. Mrs. Turner looked over her glasses while speaking to Maxine. "Ms. Gamble, I'm sorry for this visit but I needed to address the problem with you in person. We have come across some disturbing facts involving your sons. Mr. Cramer witnessed a sexual act between Myron and five female students. The art teacher asked Myron to take some supplies to another teacher, and Myron was horse playing in the hallway with the five girls in a sexual manner,"

Maxine's heart began beating fast. She didn't want to believe what the principal was saying. Maxine prayed that she could handle the problem personally without hiring a lawyer to save her son's reputation.

"Ok, Mrs. Turner, how are we going to handle this issue since Myron was behaving inappropriately with the female students?" Maxine asked as she silently prayed.

The principal wasn't willing to negotiate with Maxine. "Ms. Gamble, I'm sorry to say this but all three of your sons are expelled from school for the rest of the year. Here at Plunkett Row Academy, we do not tolerate that type of behavior."

Maxine knew she wasn't hearing the principal correctly when she heard her say all three of her sons were expelled from school for the rest of the year. Myron was the only one involved in the incident. "Did you say all three of my sons are being expelled from school based on one son's behavior?" Maxine asked as she looked the principal dead in the eye.

"Yes, Ms. Gamble, that's correct," Mrs. Turner replied as she looked over her glasses.

"Why in the world are you expelling my other two sons if they weren't involved in the sexual incident? Do you mind at least sharing with me exactly what happened?" Maxine asked while trying to keep her composure.

She wanted to get a clear picture in her head of what happened in the sexual "assault". Mrs. Turner asked Mr. Cramer to demonstrate what he witnessed.

"Mrs. Turner and Mr. Cramer, your stories don't match. Mr. Cramer said that Myron was sitting down on the bench in the hallway with five girls standing around him. You and I just watched Mr. Cramer demonstrate my son sitting on the bench with ONE of the girl's feet in between his legs. Mr. Cramer just said that Myron never touched any of the girls. Furthermore, you're expelling all three of my sons based on what again?" Maxine asked becoming offended.

 Mrs. Turner wasn't expecting to be challenged with questions, having decided already. "Ms. Gamble, I have a good reason for my decision."

"That's not making any sense to me, Mrs. Turner, because my other two sons were in class at the time you said Myron was horse playing in the hallway with the girls. You're faulting my other two sons for what reason? What time did this incident happen today? I'm getting a bit irritated," Maxine said sitting up in the chair.

"It was around 11 a.m.," Mrs. Turner said hoping that Maxine would stop questioning her and leave.

"And you wouldn't, or should I say refused to have a conference with me and the female students' parents who engaged in the incident during school hours? Before I leave here you need to understand that your staff needs some help. Mr. Cramer, don't you think it's odd to watch teenagers behave as you say they did and not stop what was going on? You said you saw this young lady grind her foot in my son's groin not once but twice. I'm going to leave and let you meditate on your decision before I take action to help you change your mind about putting my sons out of school," Maxine said. She was ready to slap the shit out of the principal and the counselor.

Mrs. Turner realized that Ms. Gamble could be a problem if not handled properly.

"We can understand that you're very upset about this matter, but there's nothing else to talk about, Ms.

Gamble. Next year your sons will be able to start with a new slate as though nothing ever happened if you decide to bring them back to Plunkett Row Academy," Mrs. Turner said trying to make light of the situation.

Maxine walked out of the principal's office very upset by Mrs. Turner's attempt to convince her that things would be okay if she just kept her sons at home for the rest of the year which was only a couple of weeks. Chance, Ahmad, and Myron were afraid when their mother walked out of the principal's office. She looked like a mad woman.

"Let's go home. I need to get some rest so that I can handle business tomorrow morning," Maxine said as they walked out of the school.

"Momma, what did the principal say we did?" Ahmad asked out of curiosity.

Maxine didn't respond because she didn't want to talk about anything as she drove. By the time Maxine arrived home, she was so stressed out that she didn't know what to do. After warming up the food in the microwave, Maxine sat with her sons at the kitchen table to pray over dinner. As Maxine passed the food around, she had to ask Myron the question that was bugging her.

"Myron, why didn't you tell me that a girl from school put her foot in between your legs?"

"Momma, I didn't think it was anything to tell since I wasn't the one who did something wrong," he responded.

I've Got to Handle This Situation

Maxine looked in the boys' room and found them all snoring like grown men. *I know I don't see a damn plate with half of a sandwich on it underneath the bed. I think it has mold on it,* Maxine thought as she walked inside their bedroom.

"Ahmad, wake your ass up and get that food from underneath your bed. If I see any bugs or a mouse around here, I'm going to beat the shit out of you," she said as she stared at her son.

Ahmad got out of bed with an innocent look on his face. Without a word, he reached under the bed and grabbed the plate he had left there three weeks earlier.

"This house better be clean when I get home from work," Maxine said as she went down the steps.

Maxine prayed that she wouldn't be late for work and that she could get her sons back in school without a fight – literally.

"I'll call Mrs. Turner's boss, the superintendent, to solve the problem," Maxine said to herself as she drove to work hoping for the best.

Maxine had typed a letter and mailed it off to the Department of Children Services asking for someone to investigate Mr. Cramer. She had a gut feeling that he didn't need to be around children. Before getting out of her car, Maxine called the superintendent of

Plunkett Row Academy. She explained the situation but didn't get the response she hoped for.

"Ms. Gamble, I've talked to Mrs. Lauran Turner about the situation, and I agree with her decision. There are only two weeks left in the school year, so your sons won't be missing out on much of anything. I only suggest that your sons be taught some morals before returning to school next year. You have a good day, Ms. Gamble. I need to be heading out for a meeting," the superintendent said before hanging up the phone.

"Hello, hello! Did this bitch just hang up in my ear?" Maxine asked herself while looking at her cell phone.

Monday Morning

The boys were enjoying their summer vacation early since being expelled from school. Chance was cooking himself breakfast while his brothers pretended to clean their rooms.

"You all better have those assignments done by the time I get home from work," Maxine said, walking out the door.

As soon as the boys heard the front door close, they turned on the television and radio to play video games and have a good time.

"Aye, go fix me a toasted peanut butter and jelly sandwich and a glass of fruit punch, Chance," Myron said as he grabbed the remote to turn the television volume up.

Chance went to the kitchen to get food for his big brother, which allowed Myron to play the video game a little longer. Ahmad begged for the controller while Chance was away.

"Here man, get yo' play on because you know when Chance comes back, he ain't goanna let you play at all," Myron said as he handed his baby brother the game controller.

Chance walked back in the room frowning up when he saw his baby brother playing the video game. Myron reached for the glass of fruit punch but lost his grip. The red drink spilled all over their mother's white lounge chair.

"Shit, Momma is going to kick my ass. It's bad enough that she's mad about what she thinks I did at school. Chance, go put some bleach water in a bucket so that I can try to clean this mess up before she gets home from work," Myron said, pushing his dreads away from his face.

The first thing on Maxine's to-do list when she got off from work was to get a written statement from Plunkett Row Academy that detailed why her sons were expelled. Trying to keep her composure, Maxine inhaled the fresh air that blew in her face as she waited to be buzzed into the school building. Maxine didn't have an appointment. She wanted the principal to be caught off guard. The secretary greeted Maxine with a smile as she walked in the central office.

"May I help you ma'am?"

"Yes, you may. Can you please inform Mrs. Turner that Ms. Gamble is here to speak with her?" Maxine asked politely.

"Sure, Ms. Gamble; have a seat while I call Mrs. Turner's office," the secretary said.

Maxine waited patiently for Mrs. Turner to appear. Ten minutes passed before Mrs. Turner showed up in the central office to greet Ms. Gamble. She looked over her glasses and wondered why the surprise visit. "Hi, Ms. Gamble, what can I do for you?"

"Well, hello Mrs. Turner. I came to get documentation for the reason all three of my sons are expelled," Maxine said trying not to show how upset she was.

Mrs. Turner was caught off guard. She didn't expect to provide anything in writing, so she quickly told a lie.

"Ms. Gamble, I gave you documentation before you left the meeting. Remember?" Mrs. Turner asked, hoping Maxine would agree then leave the school building and not return ever.

Maxine knew Mrs. Turner was lying through her cracked front teeth; and she wasn't leaving without something in writing stating why her children weren't allowed to finish the school year.

"Mrs. Turner, you and I both know that you didn't give me anything in writing when we last met. But since you think you gave me documentation, can you please give me another copy?" Maxine asked with a friendly smile.

Mrs. Turner began stuttering, saying that it wouldn't be a problem to give Maxine another copy of the document she knew she had never given her. Maxine sat with her legs crossed for an hour wondering what was taking Mrs. Turner so long to return with a copy of the letter she lied about. Mrs. Turner finally returned with a document in hand feeling a bit nervous.

 "Here's the document you requested. I hope your sons have a great summer and that we see them next year," Mrs. Turner said with a friendly smile.

Maxine read the incident report before leaving the office and stopped Mrs. Turner in her tracks.

 "Wait a minute, Mrs. Turner; this letter is implying that all three of my sons were there when this sexual incident took place, which isn't true. Also, it states that Myron slammed a door to one of the classrooms and used profanity toward Mr. Cramer as he approached him. I'm asking you as a civil-minded person to let my sons return to school, or it's going to be a bad situation for you," Maxine said as she tried to stay put in her seat to keep from harming the principal.

Mrs. Turner refused to meet Maxine's demands.

 "I'm sorry, but I can't allow your sons back in the school building this year. A fresh start next year is best, don't you think?" Mrs. Turner asked, trying to keep the staff from staring at them while discussing the matter.

"You have a good day, Mrs. Turner, because I can see that you have a personal vendetta against my family for some reason. One thing you should have done when this crazy incident occurred was to contact all the students' parents, not just me. Also, what was Mr. Cramer doing in his office when he witnessed the students doing what he claimed they were doing?" Maxine asked, giving Mrs. Turner something to think about.

Taking Action

As soon as Maxine left the school, she drove to the local police station to get things in motion to help her family. She wanted the police to investigate the incident and interrogate Mr. Cramer to make sure he wasn't a pedophile. After explaining the situation to the police officer, Maxine was advised to make the call from home to get the investigation rolling. The police officer she spoke with didn't want to lose his career by being a part of a complicated mess involving a private school. Maxine took the police officer's advice and went home.

"I'm not working overtime tonight. I just don't have the energy to deal with my co-workers," Maxine said to herself as she reached for the telephone. She sat in the middle of her bed preparing for the call.

Feeling a migraine coming on as she called her job, Maxine laid her head on her pillow until someone answered the phone. Darcey the secretary answered and hung up in Maxine's ear almost immediately when she said she wouldn't be reporting to work that night.

"Damn, is this going to be another day of people hanging up on me?" Maxine wondered, looking at the telephone.

Maxine's ringing cell phone interrupted her thoughts. It was her best friend Thelma calling to get an update on the situation with Maxine's sons.

 "Thelma, these people are trying to test my patience, and I'm about to snap on somebody seriously. Let me call the non-emergency number so that the police can come take my statement at the house. I'll call you later," Maxine said as she wiped a tear from her eye.

"Alright honey, things will work themselves out. Don't cry. If you want me to, I'll come right over," Thelma said, trying to assure her best friend that she had her support.

"You don't have to come over, Thelma. Just having you as a good friend to listen to my troubles is all I need."

"Okay, but if you change your mind, I'm just a phone call away." Thelma was concerned about her friend and wanted her to know she was there for her.

"Thanks, girlfriend. Let me get to making these phone calls so I can get some rest."

Maxine used her landline phone to call the police so that the operator would pick up her address. After speaking with the operator and expressing her troubles, Maxine was advised to be expecting the police officer within 20-30 minutes. Within 10 minutes, the police were knocking on her door.

"Hi Ms. Gamble, this is Chief Eger and I'm Officer Morris. We're here to take your statement on an incident that took place at your son's school a few days ago," Officer Morris said taking his note pad out of his pocket.

Maxine hoped to relieve some stress by reporting the incident to the police. As Maxine told the story, Officer Morris took notes to make sure he had all the crucial details.

"Ms. Gamble, we'll pay the principal a visit at school tomorrow to hear her side of the story. Then we'll get back in touch with you," Chief Eger said before leaving.

Maxine was relieved and felt things would get accomplished now that the law was involved.

Meeting with the Law

Since Maxine was confident that the police would help her, she met with a lawyer the next morning. A tall, slender, well-dressed woman in her mid-thirties greeted Maxine with a friendly smile.

"Hi, Ms. Gamble, my name is Nina Wilson. I'll be handling your case. I must say from our telephone conversation that this is an unusual case. Would you like a bottle of water or a cup of coffee?"

I'm glad someone else thinks that this is a crazy issue I'm dealing with, Maxine thought.

"No thank you, Mrs. Wilson. I just want to get this mess over with. Honestly, I feel like someone is trying to break me down emotionally. I can't explain the emotional strain. I feel so helpless, because someone is picking on my children for no reason," Maxine said with tears in her eyes.

Mrs. Wilson gently put her hand on Maxine's shoulder as they walked to the office. Maxine sat down and looked at the walls of bookshelves. She wondered what her life would have been like if she had listened to her parents and gone to college like her sister did. *I could have been a lawyer if I had totally focused on books instead of a man who I thought truly loved me,* Maxine thought.

"The first thing we can do is send a letter to the superintendent of the school to request an explanation for the expulsion. This will help us build a case against the school system if this situation makes it to court," Mrs. Wilson said taking a seat at her desk.

"Here's a copy of the incident report from the school principal," Maxine said, happy to hand the document over.

 Mrs. Wilson reviewed the incident report and couldn't believe the principal gave such incriminating information to a parent that could jeopardize so many people's careers.

Cleaning Up Your Mess

Mrs. Turner was sitting before her friend, the superintendent, sweating profusely as she thought about losing her job. "Ms. Gamble is incredibly determined to get to the bottom of the bullshit that you have created. Mr. Cramer said he watched Myron Gamble have his groin massaged by a female student with her shoe on? The police department in your district wants to have a meeting with me later this afternoon, and I want to have your story together when I tell it," Mrs. Plunkett said with anger.

"Ah ah ah, Barbie, I can explain," Mrs. Turner stuttered wiping the sweat from her forehead with her handkerchief.

"You can't explain a damn thing right now, Lauran. Ms. Gamble has hired a lawyer, which has made this problem bigger than what you could possibly imagine. Are the Gamble boys receiving any scholarship funding?" Mrs. Plunkett asked, thinking of a way to shut the problem down.

"No, they aren't under any of our scholarships directly. Ms. Gamble's employer pays 80 percent of her children's tuition through a scholarship program there," Mrs. Turner replied.

Mrs. Plunkett leaned back in her office chair trying to think of another plan of attack. "Are you going to call Child Protective Services on Ms. Gamble so that there will be an investigation of child abuse and neglect on her part? You did tell me that one of her boys has dark marks all over his body, correct? And call our friend who is employed with the IRS and make sure all her taxes are paid while you're at it. That should be enough pressure to make this woman be quiet," Mrs. Plunkett said with a sinister smile. The superintendent thought she was really going to win the battle.

Mrs. Turner was happy that her friend had come up with such a great plan.

"Yes, Myron is the one who has the marks on his arms and legs. I'll call our friend to find out if Ms. Gamble is current on her taxes so that maybe a garnishment can financially cripple her."

"By the time this Ms. Gamble gets through all the red tape, school will be closed for the summer, and we can avoid these issues. Lauran, I hope your husband isn't having an affair with Ms. Gamble and you're just taking it out on her sons. You know what happened the last time you did this with a parent you had an issue with," Mrs. Plunkett said as she looked over her glasses at her friend.

Mrs. Turner frowned remembering her husband's affair with an African American woman a parent at the school. She immediately denied that Rodger was having an affair with Maxine. "No, this isn't the case, Barbie. I can assure you. Rodger promised he would never sleep with anyone *like her* again."

Mrs. Turner turned her nose up at the thought of her husband being with another black woman.

"Ok Lauran, if I find out something different, you will be looking for employment elsewhere. My family has spent a lifetime building a great reputation for the school, and I won't let you fuck it up," Mrs. Plunkett said before dismissing Mrs. Turner from her office. Mrs. Turner left her friend relieved that she still had a job. Now she was on a mission to destroy Ms. Gamble.

Reported

Because the school system was required to report any abuse, it was easy to have a social worker start an investigation when Mrs. Turner made the call. Ms. Sky Cross, a child advocate for the state, showed up at Maxine's house after having a lengthy conversation with Mrs. Turner. Sky knocked on the door, quickly straightening her suit jacket to make her name badge visible so that she would look important. It was 12:30 in the afternoon when she showed up at the Gamble residence.

Maxine had taken the rest of the week off from work to catch up on some much-needed rest and family time. She was surprised to hear a knock at the door because she wasn't expecting any visitors. A look of concern was on Maxine's face when she opened the door to see a white woman wearing a suit and a badge.

"Hi, Ms. Gamble, my name is Sky Cross. I work for the Department of Child and Family Services. May I come in? I would like to speak with your son, Myron Gamble," Sky said with a friendly smile.

Maxine was now feeling even more confident that her troubles would soon be over after hearing Sky identify herself. It had been almost a week since Maxine had requested an investigation on the school's counselor, Mr. Cramer. The request was sent to the Department of Child Services via a certified letter. She figured Sky was there in response to her request, so she was more than happy to welcome Sky into her home.

"Sure, you can speak with my son. Please come in and have a seat. Myron is upstairs playing video games. Let me call him downstairs," Maxine said as she let the woman into her home.

Sky walked inside the apartment amazed at how well-furnished and decorated it was. She felt a bit jealous because she had a master's degree and wasn't living as well. She sat on the plush leather couch and looked at the family photos. *What do these people know about love and affection? People like them usually throw up gang signs in pictures. I bet someone had to tell them to smile,* Sky thought as she looked around.

With a fake smile, Sky asked, "What do you do for a living, Ms. Gamble?"

Myron walked in just in time. *I'm glad my baby came downstairs when he did because I was going to tell Ms. Inquiring Mind that it's none of her damn business what I do for a living. I see you Ms. Sky Cross, checking out my place when I welcomed you inside. I got my eyes on you, girlfriend. You're trying to figure out how in the world I can afford to live here with three kids. My apartment is under the low-income tax credit program, but I still end up paying regular rent at the end of the day, honey, because I work over 40 hours a week ...bitch,* Maxine thought.

"This is my son, Myron Gamble. Son, this is Ms. Cross. She works for the Department of Child and Social Services. She would like to ask you about the incident at school with the girls." Maxine was giving him the okay to tell Ms. Cross what happened.

Myron sat down in the chair across from Ms. Cross after shaking her hand.

"Ms. Gamble, do you mind giving your son and I some privacy please?" Ms. Cross asked so that she could secretly pull out her mini tape recorder.

"Yes, I do mind giving you privacy. Whatever you must ask my son you can say it in my presence," Maxine replied with her hand on her hip.

Sky gave Maxine a dirty look and then began asking questions while writing the report.

"Myron, I see that you have marks on your legs and above your right eye. Can you please tell me how you got those marks?" Sky glared at him as she asked.

Myron looked at his mother with curiosity. Maxine nodded, giving Myron permission to answer the question because it didn't bother her.

"I play football. That's how I got the mark above my eye, and I've had eczema since I was a baby. That's where the marks come from on my legs."

"Does your mother or her boyfriend ever hit you or your brothers?" Ms. Cross asked as she wrote notes of their conversation.

Maxine felt it was time to put the uninvited guest out after hearing the conversation go in a different direction.

"Sky, I suggest that you get your briefcase and get the hell out of my apartment. How dare you come in here and insinuate that my teenager is being abused?" Maxine said, pointing her finger at her.

"Ms. Gamble, I'm just doing my job. You were reported on the hotline. I had to come out to make sure that your children weren't in any danger," Ms. Cross replied as she continued to write.

"Get your shit, Sky, so that you have a chance of leaving my home unharmed," Maxine said, standing up from the living room chair.

Ms. Cross quickly grabbed her briefcase off the floor since she could see how angry Maxine was. Once she made it outside, she started saying what was on her mind.

"You'll be getting a call from my supervisor to come in the office since you ended the meeting here, Ms. Maxine Gamble."

Maxine slammed her front door with not a worry in the world.

Reply to the Law

Dear Mrs. Wilson,

I'm sending you this letter on behalf of Plunkett Row Academy in response to your letter regarding the Gamble case. The school has conducted an internal investigation and Myron, Ahmad and Chance Gamble will be suspended for the rest of the academic school year. While this case resulted in an off-campus suspension, Myron, Ahmad, and Chance Gamble will be able to take their final test to complete the academic year. Ms. Gamble is invited to contact our staff member Mr. Jaycob to arrange a time for her sons to take their finals.

Plunkett Row Academy will accept Myron, Ahmad, and Chance Gamble as students next academic school year only if Ms. Gamble signs a behavior contract. The contract will be consistent with Plunkett Row Academy's rules and will define expectations that Myron, Ahmad and Chance Gamble will need to consistently meet. These expectations include, but are not limited to, refraining from the use of inappropriate language, refraining from fighting, managing anger and aggression effectively, not engaging in any inappropriate behavior and being always respectful to others in the school. The school will send a contract prior to the start of summer school. If Ms. Gamble wishes to meet with the school administration, she is welcome to do so. Sincerely,

Mrs. B. Plunkett

Superintendent

Maxine sat in the middle of the bed in tears, after reading a copy of the letter that her lawyer received. She felt pushed two steps backwards dealing with her sons' school issues. The ringing phone interrupted Maxine's moment of depression.

"Hello stranger. Did you get a new job or what? I haven't seen you here at work and wondered how you were doing," the man on the phone said.

 "First of all, I don't know who this is. I don't recognize your phone number or your voice," Maxine replied about to hang up.

"You're speaking with Dr. Slone," he said.

Maxine dropped the phone, wondering how the doctor got her cell phone number.

She picked her cell phone up from the floor and cleared her throat.

"I'm sorry. I dropped my phone. I must say this is a surprise, Doc."

Dr. Slone smiled when he heard how excited Maxine was to hear from him.

"Maxine, it shouldn't be a surprise that I like you and would wonder how you were doing. As I said before, I haven't seen you around at work. Did you find a new job?"

"No, I didn't find a new job. I'm just going through some personal issues that need my attention."

"Understood. Is there anything I can do to help?"

Maxine took a minute to think of something Dr. Slone could do for her but drew a blank.

"There's nothing you can do to help me out, but thanks for asking. I was about to go to sleep just before you called. I thank you for being concerned about me. We'll talk some other time, ok?" Maxine said wanting to end the conversation.

"Don't hang up please, Maxine. I don't know if I'll ever get the courage to ask this question again. Will you please allow me to take you out for dinner?"

"Dr. Slone, you're very persistent but I must decline. There are many female co-workers that would love for you to take them out in a heartbeat. I'm not an easy lay, so I suggest you stop trying to get my attention," Maxine said with an attitude.

She figured Dr. Slone was up to no good, so she was purposely killing his ego.

"The thought of you as an easy lay never crossed my mind. I just wanted to have some quality time with you over dinner. How about we just go out for coffee tomorrow morning since you're declining my offer for dinner?" Dr. Slone said jokingly.

"Ok, only coffee. Do you know where Blueberry Star Coffee Cafe is?"

"Yes, as a matter of fact I do, Maxine."

"Meet me there at 8:30 a.m."

"See you then and I hope things get better for you. Good night."

Maxine smiled at the thought of Dr. Slone hunting her down just to talk to her and ask for a date. *Now why did I agree to have coffee with Dr. Slone? What are we really going to talk about other than what's going on at work?* Maxine thought before falling asleep.
Tossing and turning in bed, Maxine just couldn't rest. The stress of everything had her stomach in knots. She didn't fall asleep until around 4 a.m.

Ahmad greeted Maxine a little after 8 a.m. with bacon and cheese on wheat toast, a cup of coffee, and the morning paper on a serving tray.

 "Momma, wake up. I cooked breakfast for you. Here's a cup of hot coffee with just sugar the way you like it," he said.

Maxine smiled when she rolled over in bed and saw Ahmad holding the serving tray. Ahmad was the spitting image of his father. He was average height for a young man with brown complexion and hazel eyes.

 "Ahmad, what are you up to now? Why are you serving me breakfast in bed?"

"Well, it's been a week since we got suspended from school and playing video games every day has gotten boring. We were wondering if we could go over to Tyson's house to hangout for the weekend. Auntie is giving him a pool party on Saturday so we thought it would be cool if we just stayed over the whole weekend. Please, please, please, Momma," Ahmad begged. Ahmad and his brothers really wanted to spend the weekend at their auntie's house to get better acquainted with the girls that just moved in the neighborhood.

Maxine gave it some thought while eating breakfast.

"Ok, tell your brothers that you all can spend the night at your Auntie Eva's house, but Auntie Eva must bring you all back home by Sunday morning. We're going to church as a family," she said before sipping the hot coffee.

"Ok, Momma," Ahmad said with a huge smile spread across his face. He reached over and hugged his mother and then ran out of the room to tell his brothers the good news.

I have a coffee date in two minutes, and I haven't even showered yet, Maxine thought when she realized what time it was as she finish eating her breakfast. Maxine grabbed her phone and called the number Dr. Slone called her from the evening before.

"Good morning," Dr. Slone said answering on the first ring.

"Good morning, Dr. Slone; I'm sorry to be the bearer of bad news, but I'm not going to be able to meet you this morning. I just woke up and realized what time it was," she said, telling a little fib.

"What about dinner then since you're cancelling our morning coffee date? I'm sitting at Blueberry Star Café, and I see a place across the street that I think you'll like."

"Ok, I'll have dinner with you only if it's in the early evening – say around 6:00," she suggested.

"See you then, Maxine."

Getting Ready for the Date

Thelma stopped by to check on Maxine, because she hadn't talked to her in a few days. She wanted to make sure everything was alright with her. Sitting on the edge of Maxine's bed, Thelma admired the fifth outfit her friend tried on.

"That's a cute outfit, but I must admit it's sending a silent message that the doctor is getting some ass tonight. You might as well put on them five-inch heels to match the dress," Thelma smirked.

"I'm not wearing the dress or the five-inch heels, because Dr. Slone ain't getting nothing tonight. You know it's been a long time since I've been out on a date, so I appreciate the truth," Maxine answered, going back into her walk-in closet to find a different outfit.

"How's the school situation coming along?"

"Let's change the subject, Thelma. I'm trying to keep the school situation off my mind for now and concentrate on what the hell I'm going to be talking about with Dr. Slone," Maxine muttered as she stood looking at herself in another outfit.

"Ok next question, how in the world did you and Dr.

Slone arrange this dinner date? Let's talk about that, and I'm not changing the subject until you give me an answer, Ms. Gamble."

Maxine laughed as she put on a green Gucci jumpsuit with a pair of three-inch Jimmy Choo snakeskin pumps. She grabbed a gold leather wristlet and put her driver's license and lipstick in it. Maxine gave herself a nod of approval in the mirror before addressing Thelma.

"Dr. Slone has been after me for some time. He probably thinks he's going to get some ass. Conversation with a smile is all I'm putting on the platter for him tonight."

"I'm your friend, Maxine; now be for real. How long have you and Doc been messing around?" Thelma asked thinking her best friend had been withholding a secret.

"You're going to make me late for my dinner date. Here are your car keys. Come on so I can get out of here," Maxine said avoiding the trivia questions.

She wanted to be on time. Maxine walked Thelma to the front door, gave her a hug and pushed her out of the apartment. Easing into the soft leather seat of her car, Maxine felt butterflies in her stomach before starting the engine. *I'm just going to hang out with the opposite sex, have a good time and then come right back home.*
What if one of our co-workers sees us out?

Shit, I'm grown. Hell, who cares what people say?

Here goes nothing, Maxine thought as she took a deep breath and started her car. When Maxine backed out of the garage, Thelma was waiting for her on the sidewalk.

"Have a good time, Maxine! Don't deprive yourself of shit! You hear me? Order everything on the damn menu, because you know Dr. Slone can afford it," Thelma said, cracking up laughing before getting into her car.

Maxine just shook her head and waved goodbye to her best friend. She knew Thelma didn't have a bit of good damn sense.

The Date

Dr. Slone sat in the cozy restaurant hoping not to be stood up twice in the same day by Maxine. He ordered a second round of drinks to calm his nerves, thinking of what to say when he saw her. The waitress took Dr. Slone's order for the drinks and walked away with a smile. Maxine walked into the restaurant in a hurry to get the date over with and get back home. Once she spotted her co-worker, she strutted toward him like a runway model in a fashion show. All eyes were on Maxine because she had it going on. Her hips swayed slightly from side to side as she walked. She smelled good and looked fresh.

"Hey Doc," Maxine said, trying not to be so formal.

"Well, hello, Maxine. I'm delighted that you came."

Dr. Slone stood up to give Maxine a friendly hug, but she took a step back. Instead of reacting to the rejection, Dr. Slone held Maxine's chair out and invited her to sit down before joining her at the table.

"I took the liberty of ordering dinner and drinks. I hope you will like what I chose. You told me you eat pretty much all types of food," Dr. Slone said as he looked directly at her.

Maxine didn't put up a fuss because she was willing to indulge and eat something different. The waitress served their salads and wine while Maxine admired the ambience.

"It's funny how you can pass by a place for years and then visit just to find out you've been missing out on something. This restaurant is nice," Maxine said before putting a fork full of salad in her mouth.

When the waitress served the entrees, Maxine was puzzled. She didn't recognize what Dr. Slone had ordered for her to eat.

"Excuse me, miss, but can you please tell me what this is?" Maxine asked the waitress.

"Sure ma'am. You have broiled chicken with cranberry green bean sauce and steamed broccoli glazed in coconut butter," the waitress replied with a friendly smile.

The waitress was a 'sista' that knew black folks mostly ate foods they could recognize. The food on Maxine's plate looked more like art. *If Dr. Slone thinks I'm eating this mess he's crazy. I could have eaten chicken at home,* Maxine thought as she looked at the food and contemplated at least trying it.

"I would like to order something different please. You can take this plate of food back to the kitchen. I would like grilled salmon and asparagus with brown rice," Maxine said as she handed the plate back to the waitress.

The waitress looked over at Dr. Slone to get his approval to change the order, because she had seen some crazy situations happen in the elegant restaurant.

"Yes ma'am; will there be anything else for you, sir?" the waitress asked.

"I'm fine; get whatever the lady wants. Thank you," Dr. Slone said, signaling his approval for the change.

Maxine didn't have anything to say to Dr. Slone until the other meal arrived. The waitress returned quickly with Maxine's new order.

"Will there be anything else, ma'am?" the waitress asked, trying to provide elite service in exchange for a decent tip.

"No thank you; I'll be fine with this," Maxine replied.

She focused her attention back to Dr. Slone once the server walked away.

"So, Dr. Slone, why are you pursuing me?"

"I think you're a beautiful person, Maxine, and I'd like to get to know you better," he answered, being honest.

"I'm flattered, but I know for a fact anyone of the single nurses that I work with would love to be in my shoes right now. They'd love to hear you compliment them."

Dr. Slone motioned gently with his hand. "I am aware of some of the ladies with hopes to marry any available doctor at the hospital, but I'm interested in a woman like you. Can you call me Chad from now on when we're outside of work?"

Maxine kept on eating her food and sipping her wine as the doctor spoke. Dr. Slone's conversation was making her feel a certain kind of way. She loved the forwardness of a man who knew what he wanted.

 "Dr. Slone, I mean Chad, I have a lot going on in my life with such little time to waste. The dinner was delicious, but I must be going in a few minutes. I have a couple of errands to run before returning home," she said, wanting to end the date early and get some needed rest.

"Maxine, your time with me will always be spent wisely. It will never be wasted. This evening is the beginning of time well spent between us; don't you think?"

The man was persistent, but Maxine had to be honest with him. "Chad, I don't date outside of my race and don't think I ever will."

She couldn't deal with the stress of an interracial relationship right now. Maxine wasn't prejudice, but she didn't want stares and talks behind her back that would come from her dating a white man. She was raised in the hood, and some of the things learned from her upbringing would never change. Dr. Slone didn't understand why Maxine made such a crazy statement about race and didn't hesitate to correct her.

"I'm African American, Maxine, but if I were Caucasian why would it even matter?" Dr. Slone asked with curiosity.

"Race matters to me because people still have problems with interracial couples in the twentieth century. Do you see how people are staring at us right now?" she asked, pointing to a couple across the restaurant looking in their direction.

"Maxine, people are staring because we are two nice looking people sitting together minding grown folks' business," Dr. Slone replied with a grin.

Maxine smiled as she discovered that Dr. Slone had a little sense of humor. By the time the bottle of wine was empty, the two were laughing and touching hands from across the table like they were longtime friends.

Gossip

Thelma was ringing Maxine's telephone at 7 a.m. Saturday morning wanting to know what happened on her best friend's date with Dr. Slone. Maxine wasn't up to talking that early in the morning on her day off.

"Thelma, please call me back around 1 p.m. I got a hangover out of this world," Maxine said, trying to get off the phone.

"One question before I hang up: is Dr. Slone in the bed beside you right now?"

Maxine had to laugh at her friend.

"Girl, bye. I'll call you later, Thelma. I promise."

Maxine rolled over to go back to sleep.

Thirty minutes later, someone was knocking and ringing Maxine's doorbell.

"Shit, who could possibly be at my door?" Maxine grumbled.

She slid out of bed, holding her pounding head. The knocking on the door made Maxine's head hurt even worse.

"Now since you wouldn't tell me over the telephone how your date went, I came in person to find out," Thelma said as she walked past Maxine to get in the apartment. Maxine gave her best friend a slight smile as they walked into the kitchen together. "Sit down! I'll make coffee while you tell me everything," Thelma demanded looking inside the fridge for some creamer before turning on the coffee maker.

Maxine laid her head on the kitchen table as Thelma moved around the kitchen like she lived there. After Thelma poured them both a cup of coffee and handed Maxine a piece of dry toast, she sat down to hear about the date with Dr. Slone.

"Start talking, girl," Thelma said with a devilish smile.

"Dr. Slone, I mean Chad, is a nice guy. One thing he did that rubbed me the wrong way in the beginning of our date was that he ordered dinner for me that wasn't worth ordering. It turned out to be broiled chicken with sauce I've never heard of. It didn't look appealing enough to put in my mouth. We had small talk about a lot of things that have happened in our lives. Then we made plans to have a second date in two weeks. That's the end of the story," Maxine said before putting a piece of toast in her mouth.

Thelma didn't want to hear about what they ate for dinner. She wanted to hear that Maxine was eaten for dessert and the rest of the nasty things she would have done if given the chance to be with Dr. Slone herself. "What Maxine? I was thinking you were going to have an X-rated story that I could visualize, but I'm going to give you your props for sticking to your guns and not giving up the ass the first night. Y'all calling each other by first names, huh? So where are you two going on the next date? Will it be dinner and dancing at his place?" Thelma asked, being nosey.

"No dinner or dancing at his place and, yes, we are on a first name basis. Chad isn't as stuck up as I thought he would be. He also told me that he's black. I thought he was joking until he showed me a few pictures of his parents on his cell phone. Chad has an African American mother and a French father who he resembles a whole lot. Most of his family lives in New Orleans where he was raised," Maxine said with a smile thinking about Dr. Slone.

"Wow! Dr. Slone can pass for something other. I say you better hook his ass in a relationship before one of them nurses strike gold and gets his undivided attention. It's been a long time since a man smashed that ass of yours, so I say give it a chance. You're not getting any younger, and God has kept you looking youthful," Thelma blurted out snapping her fingers in the air.

"I'm just doing something to pass the time. A relationship isn't what I'm looking for right now, and Chad understands this," Maxine explained as she looked at her best friend.

Thelma looked at Maxine as though she wasn't making good sense of the good advice she was giving her.

Assuming

Maxine complied with the school's policy and had a time scheduled for her sons to take their final exams. As soon as she walked in the school's central office with her sons, one of the staff members pointed at them and whispered to her co-worker. "Look, those are the boys that engaged in touching those girls a few weeks ago," she said.

Maxine told her sons to turn around and go back to the car, because she could see she still had a major problem with the school system disrespecting her family. She went back to the police department to check on the progress with the investigation. Maxine parked her car and warned her sons before getting out that there would be trouble for them if they misbehaved while she was inside. Office Morris noticed Maxine as soon as she walked into the building and tried to get out of sight before he was spotted.

"Officer Morris! Officer Morris!" Maxine called as he tried to escape to an empty holding room to avoid her.

"Hi Ms. Gamble, what can I do for you?" Officer Morris asked sarcastically.

"I would like to know if there has been any progress on the investigation since last week. I took my sons to take their finals, and I'm still dealing with the drama," Maxine said in a frustrated tone.

"Ms. Gamble, there was a meeting with the principal and superintendent of the school, and they promised us that they would handle the problem with you appropriately," Officer Morris said, trying to end their conversation.

"I understand now what's going on, Officer Morris. Can you give me a copy of your report stating that?" Maxine asked as she tried to keep her composure, yet again.

"There is no report to be given, Ms. Gamble. The Chief and I only had a discussion with Mrs. Turner, and we will not take the matter any further," Officer Morris said. He was getting a little agitated with Maxine at that point because she hadn't left the building.

"Can you write down that there will be no further investigation dealing with my son's case?" Maxine asked while keeping her composure in tack.

She needed evidence that the police department refused to investigate her sons' case and deal with the private school. Frustrated, Officer Morris snatched a flyer off the counter and wrote on the back of it. *After our investigation last week, the police department will not pursue anything further.*

Ms. Gamble will have to handle her problem with the school system using other representation, he wrote. Then he signed his name along with his badge number on the back of the flyer. Maxine stuffed the paper in her purse and told Officer Morris to have a good day before leaving the building. She assumed that the principal must have told Chief Eger and Officer Morris something negative to be treated in such of a way.

Maxine drove her son's home.

"You all warmup those leftovers and study for your finals until I get back," Maxine said when she pulled up in front of the apartment building.

The boys got out of the car without saying a word, knowing their mother was terribly upset after leaving the police station.

Headquarters

When Maxine walked into the police headquarters, she was greeted by a tall, dark, and handsome officer dressed in uniform.

 "Can I help you with something ma'am?" the officer asked.

Maxine tried to ignore how handsome the policeman was.

"How can I file a complaint against a police officer?" Maxine asked trying to stay focused on the reason why she was there.

The officer pointed toward the Internal Affairs Office with a displeased look on his face. *I don't care what you think, officer. I'm a mother trying to protect my damn kids,* Maxine thought as she walked down the hallway. When Maxine walked in the office of Internal Affairs, she was greeted by the secretary, an elderly woman in her mid-seventies.

"Good morning. May I help you, ma'am?"

"Good morning, I'm in need of some assistance with filing a complaint against a police officer," Maxine explained hoping that the woman could assist her.

 The elderly woman called for one of the detectives to come up front to assist Maxine. After hearing the reason why Maxine wanted to file the complaint against the police officer, the detective had her wait in the lobby area while he got hold of the Chief of Police. Damn near shaking in his boots after having a conversation with Chief Eger, Detective Norman returned and asked Maxine to come with him while he documented her complaint. Maxine walked past a group of police officers and detectives that stared at her strangely, because they already knew what she was there for. Being as honest as she could be, Maxine summarized the entire ordeal: from the day she met Officer Morris and Chief Eger coming to her house about the school's sexual allegations against her sons to the exchange she had just had with Officer Morris.

Filing the complaint against Officer Morris was more of a hassle than Maxine thought it would be. The detective stepped away to make a few more phone calls. Maxine watched closely as the detective delayed giving her a copy of the paperwork. Thanks to her patience, by the time she left police headquarters, she finally received documentation that her matter would be investigated further.

Night Shift

Maxine dreaded working the night shift that night because she hadn't gotten any rest that day. She was polite when she walked into the break room. Maxine spoke to everyone, but nobody responded. The night staff did not know her, so they didn't feel like they needed to befriend her for eight hours just because she volunteered to work on their unit overtime. Maxine sat quietly with the rest of the staff to receive their assignment and listen to the nightly report. *I hope to see another patient care tech soon or it's going to be a long night,* Maxine thought. After listening to the recorded report, the charge nurse broke the bad news to Maxine.

"Maxine, you're the only patient care technician working until 2 a.m. I called the staffing office and was informed that another patient care tech will be pulled from another floor." The charged nurse flashed a fake ass smile.

Maxine responded with just an "okay" and left the break room to start taking vitals on all 32 patients while the nurses stayed behind laughing and listening to rock music.

When she was finished taking vitals on the patients and charting the information in the computer, her pager began to beep like crazy.

104A needs a stat PTT blood drawn and the patient in 101 needs to use the bed pan. 110 needs an extra blanket, the messages read. *Damn, can a nurse draw the blood on the patient in room 104 bed A while I go help the patient with the bed pan? I'm the only tech working the floor, and I don't see a nurse in sight,* Maxine thought as she stood at the nurse's station alone.

As Maxine was about to print out her own label to draw blood on the patient in room 104 bed A, she heard someone laughing in the break room. Out of curiosity, she peeked inside of the break room to see which employees were still sitting on their asses 'lollygagging' around. Yet again, same shit on a different work shift. A few of the nurses were passing pictures around of their vacation and eating pizza – after only giving pills to their patients since clocking in for work. *I am going to find me another job as soon as I get a chance. I'm too old to be dealing with this bullshit,* Maxine thought as she helped all the patients listed in the text messages.

Another Meeting

Maxine walked in the house glad to be home after that eight-hour night shift by herself. All she wanted to do was take a shower and go to sleep. The boys were sleeping and unaware that their mother had returned home from work.

As she let the warm water of the shower spray down on her body, she massaged her clitoris slowly until she was relaxed. She yearned for a man's touch. Caressing her breast with one hand, she grabbed the shower head attachment, put her right foot on the edge of the bathtub and let the water hit the right spot.

"Let me get out of here and go to bed," Maxine whispered to herself in a low tone.

Still feeling horny, Maxine locked her bedroom door, lit a few candles, and grabbed her joy toy Mr. Mix to satisfy her needs. Maxine's joy toy was all that she needed right before going to bed. It was six inches long, thick and stayed hard all the time. Maxine had no complaints about her great investment. The flickering from the candles made her wish a man was there beside her.

As Luther Vandross came through the speakers of her stereo, Maxine laid in the middle of the bed with her eyes closed and pretended that a masculine man was taking control of her body and holding her tight. She pinched herself hard, erect nipples with her right hand as she held Mr. Mix with the left. She allowed her joy toy to go in and out of her body. As she got close to an orgasm, Maxine fantasized about the days when Oliver used to hump her like a dog in heat.

"Oooh shit, this feels so good," she moaned.

Maxine was so deep in thought and grinding Mr. Mix so hard that she had to make herself stop before she gave herself an infection. She got out of bed to wash Mr. Mix, blew out the candles and then crawled in the bed to go peacefully to sleep.

Up In Time

Maxine woke up at 3:30 p.m. by the ringing of the telephone. "Hi Maxine, this is Mrs. Wilson. I just wanted to let you know that I will be a little late getting to the Child Advocacy Center today. I'm held up here in court, but I advise you not to talk too much. Also, please don't sign anything without me being present," Mrs. Wilson said with hopes that her client understood her clearly.

"Ok, see you soon," Maxine said, agreeing to do as Mrs. Wilson suggested.

Later that afternoon, Maxine stood in front of the massive red brick building, took a deep breath, and silently prayed that peace would be upon the people who had control to do the right thing for her children. A short Caucasian woman was sitting at the desk when Maxine entered the building with her family.

"Hello, are you Ms. Gamble?" the woman asked as Maxine closed the front door.

"Yes, I am Ms. Gamble. I have a meeting with the detective and the social worker from the Department of Children and Social Services at 5:30. My lawyer should be coming shortly. These are my sons Chance, Ahmad, and Myron Gamble," she said with a friendly smile.

The boys greeted the woman and then sat down in the lobby picking up the car and video game magazines to read.

"It's a pleasure to meet your family. My name is Sanoma. I'm one of the child advocates who will be conducting the meeting with you and your family. The detective and the social worker will be speaking mainly with Myron to hear his side of the story about the incident that occurred at the school. Would you like to begin our session while your sons sit in the lobby? It's not necessary to wait on your lawyer. She won't be allowed to go in the room when we speak with you or your son," Sanoma said kindly.

"I'd rather wait until my lawyer gets here before we begin the meeting, please," Maxine said, smiling right back at Sanoma.

The detective from police headquarters arrived at the Child Advocacy Center at 5:15 p.m. The social worker from the state arrived less than 10 minutes later. By 5:50 p.m. Maxine was wondering where in the hell Mrs. Wilson was. The detective spoke briefly with Sanoma and the social worker in the other room and then returned to speak with Maxine.

"Ms. Gamble, can we begin the meeting? I have another appointment in about 30 minutes," the detective asked with a stern look on his face.

Maxine looked at her watch. It was now 6:15 p.m. She decided to begin the meeting without Mrs.

Wilson being present, thinking that her lawyer must still be in court. Maxine didn't want to waste any more time. The detective was glad to work his "male magic" on Maxine to get this necessary meeting over with.

"Sure, we can begin, sir. My lawyer may not be able to make it in time, but I want to put this issue to rest," Maxine said as she told Myron to go with the social worker and detective and to be honest when answering their questions.

Myron walked upstairs behind the social worker and the detective into one room. Maxine reluctantly went into the room next door with Sanoma to be interrogated.

"Have a seat, Ms. Gamble. Can I get you a bottle of water before we begin?" Sanoma asked with a friendly smile.

"No, thank you," Maxine answered, feeling a bit uncomfortable.

"Ok, my questions to you will be really simple ones," Sanoma said, trying to assure Maxine that everything was going to be all right.

Maxine just stared and waited to be questioned with the hopes that Mrs. Wilson would be arriving any minute. "Ms. Gamble, what is the highest level of education you have completed?" Sanoma asked preparing to enter the answers in the computer.

"I completed one year of college, ma'am," Maxine replied dryly.

"Are you employed, Ms. Gamble?"

"Yes, I'm employed, ma'am."

"Do you mind telling me where you're employed, Ms. Gamble?"

"At one of the best hospitals located in Saint Louis city," Maxine quickly answered with trying to figure out why Sanoma was asking so many questions about her personal life.

Sanoma stopped asking questions briefly while entering the information into the computer with a few personal opinions.

"Do you receive any assistance from the government, Ms. Gamble?" Sanoma asked, hoping Maxine would say yes.

This is some more bullshit, Maxine thought.

"Have you ever been sexually molested?" Sanoma asked, looking over her glasses.

"Look lady, I'm not crazy. I come from a two-parent household and have never been the victim of any type of sexual abuse. This meeting is over," Maxine said standing to her feet to leave and go get Myron.

As Maxine walk out of the room, Mrs. Wilson walked up the stairs, hoping it wasn't too late to help her client.

"Ms. Gamble, where's Myron? I saw Chance and Ahmad downstairs," she said with a look of concern.

Maxine walked past Mrs. Wilson and Sanoma to end Myron's private meeting with the detective and the State social worker, but it was too late. They had all the information they needed. Myron was coached by the social worker to say that the girl who had placed her shoe on his groin area was only horse playing with him. They coached him to say it wasn't in a sexual manner as the school counselor said.

"Ms. Gamble, we videotaped our meeting with Myron. Can we use this footage for our law students since it is such an unusual case?" the social worker asked.

"Hell, no you can't use my case for shit without my permission, and if I ever find out about it, I'm suing."

Maxine turned to her son. "Let's go Myron!"

She walked down the steps mad as hell.

Maxine had never been in trouble in her life and had a feeling the police department and school system were up to no good. It seemed they wanted to bring her and her children down so she would keep quiet about the school incident.

Confusion

Two days before the last day of school, Ahmad, Chance, and Myron were accepted to take their finals without negativity from the school staff upon entering the building. Around that same time, Maxine received a letter of apology from the superintendent of Plunkett Row Academy.

Dear Ms. Gamble,

We at Plunkett Row Academy would like to apologize for the misunderstanding on our part. Myron, Chance, and Ahmad Gamble are being sponsored for their education until their high school graduation date. Along with this letter are three applications for the scholarships. Please return the applications as soon as possible.

Congratulations,

Mrs. B. Plunkett

So, this is their way of apologizing after putting me through emotional hell? Too many people were going to lose their job because someone had a problem with me or my children, Maxine thought as she put the letter and applications in the trash.

Mrs. Wilson sat in her office reading a copy of the letter Maxine received from the private school board. She thought back to the day of Maxine's meeting at the Children's Advocacy Center. On the way to that meeting, Mrs. Wilson had not only gotten held up in court. Right after, she was in a car accident. She ended up having to catch a cab to meet her client that day.

Mrs. Wilson knew Maxine had the opportunity for a hell of a lawsuit based on defamation of character and harassment alone. This lawsuit would have put her law career on easy street. Knowing the law, Mrs. Wilson knew why the detective had Myron's interview on tape to keep for evidence. It was so that Maxine couldn't sue and say her son was molested by any of the female students at the private school during school hours – and with the school counselor as witness.

Ironically, Mrs. Wilson knew if the genders were reversed and a teenage boy had put his foot in a female's groin area at school, the police would have been called along with the female's parents. There would have been a report of some sort filed on behalf of the female student. The boy's parent would have been notified once their son had been locked up in a juvenile detention facility, and you can imagine the rest of the turnout.

In a nutshell, Officer Morris, Chief Eger, Mr. Cramer the school counselor, and good ole Principal Turner who helped create the lie that blew up into a big mess could all have been fired.

Maxine found out later that her boys were targeted because she had rubbed Mrs. Galton, the assistant principal, the wrong way. Mrs. Galton's name was never mentioned during the whole ordeal until she talked about Maxine to the wrong staff member. When Maxine enrolled the boys at the beginning of the school year and paid the deposit on their tuition, she was questioned about how she could afford private school and drive a fancy car when she was a single parent of three kids.

After Maxine politely told Mrs. Galton it was none of her business and that she made an honest living, Mrs. Galton was angry and sought revenge for the disrespect. Once the truth was revealed, Mrs. Galton, Mrs. Turner, and Mr. Cramer lost their jobs the following school year.

Scared to Take a Leap of Faith

Dr. Slone was happy to get more of Maxine's quality time since her problems with the school were over. During the workday, they would meet for lunch at a nearby cafe to learn more about each other. One day, Maxine decided to share some of her personal information with Dr. Slone.

"Chad, I need to tell you why I'm putting my education on hold. I'm the mother of three handsome boys. They're 15, 14 and 12. I tried attending college after graduating from high school but couldn't handle it and family life at the same time," Maxine said feeling a little disappointed in herself.

Maxine waited for Dr. Slone to make up an excuse to leave after now finding out she was a mother of, not only one, but three children.

"Being a parent is even more of a motivation to accomplish your goals if you ask me, Maxine. So how old were you when you had your first child if you don't mind me asking with *yo* fine self?" Dr. Slone asked as he winked at her.

"I was fourteen when I gave birth to my first child. My parents both worked day and night. They were more involved in running their church than keeping a watchful eye on me. The only concerns my parents had once they found out I was pregnant was finding out who the father was so that his family could pay for an abortion. By the time my third child was born, my parents threatened to kick me out of the house. So one day I left on my own after saving up enough money," Maxine said, thinking back on that day.

"Do all of your children have the same father?" Dr. Slone asked, just to be nosey.

"I'm proud to say that all three of my boys are with the same man. There was something about Oliver, my children's father, that kept me running to him no matter how much wrong he had done toward me and my family," Maxine admitted.

"Maxine, we're adults. Don't be ashamed. You and I both know what kept you going back to the father of your children. So, is he in your sons' lives?"

Maxine smiled when she reminisced about the things she used to do sexually with Oliver.

"Oliver is a great father and is very active in our sons' lives," Maxine replied, happy to admit.

"You are in such great physical shape to have three teenagers," he said, admiring her natural beauty.

"Let's not forget, I just told you I was a 14-year-old kid having kids now. Stop it with the compliments Doc." Maxine looked at her watch and noticed it was time to return to work. She didn't want to get in trouble for not returning from her lunch break on time.

"Let's get back to work before I get the evil eye from my co-workers," Maxine said as she reached over and rubbed the doctor's hand.

She stood up and dusted off a few crumbs that fell into her lap. Meanwhile, Dr. Slone looked her over from head to toe before walking back to the hospital from one of the restaurants in the Central West End area.

As soon as Maxine returned to the floor, her pager started to vibrate. ***There will be a mandatory staff meeting in the break room at three o'clock,*** the message read. Maxine was hoping that the staff meeting wasn't going to last past 4:30, because she had plans after work and didn't want to be late.

Ms. Hyson, the nursing supervisor, asked Peggy to pass around a stack of pamphlets before the meeting began.

"Ladies, thank you for attending the meeting. Please sign the sign-in sheet to get paid for your attendance. The dress code is changing throughout the hospital. Patients are mistaking patient care technicians as nurses, because some of you wear all white or navy blue. Also, the patients can't see the title on our badges, and that is a problem."

Ms. Hyson continued, "On July 1, patient care technicians must start wearing burgundy uniforms. Please sign the form that's passed around to acknowledge that you understand the changes to the dress code. If you are not in proper uniform, you will be written up without a warning. Nurses are to wear all white or navy blue. The registered nurse badges will have 'RN' in bold lettering under their full name. The licensed practical nurses will have 'LPN' in bold lettering on their badges above their full name. The patient care technicians will have PCT up top then their full name on the badge," the supervisor said with a friendly smile.

Maxine assumed Peggy had something to do with the dress code changes but didn't let it get under her skin, because she knew she looked good in anything she wore. Ready to go and 'get the hell out of dodge', Maxine signed the sign-in sheet and the dress code enforcement form, and then told everyone goodbye.

It's Friday

Maxine was sitting in her car relieved to be off work. She decided to call Thelma since it was her best friend's birthday.

 "I thought you forgot all about me," Thelma said joking around.

"Now come on Thelma; everyone in the world knows you were born today. Didn't you post it on every one of the social media platforms?" Maxine said laughing her ass off.

Thelma laughed along with her best friend.

"I'll come pick you up around 7:30. Is that cool with you? I just got off work and need to take a shower," Maxine said while driving home and rocking her head to the beat of the music playing in the background.

"Take as much time as you need. I just want to have a fun time for my birthday with my best friend," Thelma said, getting all excited.

Maxine had made special plans for Thelma's birthday a month in advance. She was hoping Thelma would be pleased on her special day. Chance, Ahmad, and Myron hopped up off the couch when they heard their mother's keys turning in the lock of the front door. Maxine walked in the living room and saw candy wrappers and soda cans on the floor. Her sons tried to look busy cleaning up the mess.

"There's no need to pretend. I know doggone well you all haven't been playing video games all damn day in my living room. I'm going out tonight, and you all are going over to your Auntie Eva's house in half an hour. Go pack an overnight bag so that you all will be ready when she comes to pick you up."

"Momma, don't you think we're old enough to stay at home alone? Every time you get ready to go someplace you want us to go over to Auntie Eva's house, or you pay someone to watch us. We are teenagers," Myron pleaded as he unhooked the video game console's wires from the living room TV.

Maxine gave a look that only her sons understood. Immediately, the boys started cleaning up their mess as fast as they could, so they could pack their overnight bags.

Birthday Girl

Thelma was really surprised that Maxine had laid out the red carpet for her birthday celebration. She felt special and appreciated by her dear friend. "Look at your girl about to pass out on the dance floor. Good thing they're slow dancing. That dude is holding her drunk ass up!" Genevieve said. Genevieve was Maxine and Thelma's co-worker.

"You're just mad no one is holding your jealous ass up on the dance floor, Genevieve. If you came here to kill Thelma's good vibe, I suggest you leave and take that bad energy with you," Maxine said popping her fingers to the music.

One thing Maxine didn't like was a female trying to create some childish shit for no reason. She had reserved the largest V.I.P. section at the club and had ordered Thelma a beautiful birthday cake. There was plenty of food and drinks for the guests invited to have a good time. Maxine and Thelma took pictures at the photo booth striking a sexy pose. Then the two friends went back to their table to take snapshots with family and friends as the crowd wished Thelma a happy birthday.

Thelma wore a hot pink, glow-in-the-dark, spandex body suit that had men's heads turning. As soon as

they walked into the club, one man claimed that
Thelma was going to be his woman for the night.
Thelma didn't put up a fight because she thought the
man was rather nice looking.

Party's Over

Later that night, Thelma wanted Maxine to go across the bridge to East St. Louis where the clubs stayed opened 6 a.m. Maxine thought it was a bad idea and was tired from working all day. Thelma's newfound male companion volunteered to drive her anywhere she wanted to go if she agreed to spend the night with him. As Thelma walked toward the man's car, Maxine grabbed her by the arm.

"Thelma, get your drunk ass in my car before we end up fighting in this parking lot. You are not going with this stranger that you've only known for four hours. We came here together, and we are going home together," Maxine said, making herself clear.

Thelma laughed at Maxine's comment then reached to hug her newfound man friend for showing her a fun time for her birthday.

"I'm going home with my best friend. Let me give you my phone number so you can call me some time," Thelma said to the man while licking her lips.

Thelma's newfound man companion was disappointed with her decision to leave with Maxine. He had spent money on drinks for Thelma all night and wanted to be paid back with sex. He tried to convince her. Meanwhile, Maxine argued with Thelma, reminding her that she didn't even know the man's name she had been entertaining all night.

Thelma leaned over to whisper to the man to get his name and got a whiff of his stank ass breath. *'Got damn'! What in the hell died in this man's mouth?* Thelma thought as she backed away from the man and got into Maxine's car. The man tapped on the car window signaling for Thelma to roll it down.

 "Can you at least give me a kiss for showing you a good time on your birthday, baby girl?"

"Drive away, Maxine. This man doesn't practice good enough hygiene to brush his teeth, and up here asking to exchange bodily fluids!" Thelma exclaimed as she turned up her nose shaking her head.

Maxine laughed as she drove away, leaving the man in the nightclub parking lot with his hands up in the air.

Next Day

Maxine woke up the next morning to the sounds of Thelma throwing up in a bucket beside the bed. *I knew my girl couldn't handle her liquor*; she thought as she listened to her friend puking. Maxine got out of bed and went to the bathroom to shit, shower, and get dressed to run her errands. Wishing that she would feel better, Thelma laid wrapped up in Chance's bed hoping that her head would stop spinning.

  "Thelma, I have errands to run, so stay in bed to recuperate until I come back. I'll cook you something when I return. There is a pot of coffee downstairs whenever you are ready to drink it."

"Okay girl, thank you so much. I'm going to stay right here in Chance's bed until you come back home. My head is still spinning like crazy. If I stay till la…" Thelma threw up again before she could finish her sentence. Maxine left the room, grabbed her purse and keys and headed out the front door hoping Thelma would be okay until she returned.

While in the grocery store, Maxine ended up buying more than what was on her list. *That is what happens when I come to the grocery store hungry,* she thought while putting the bags in the car. After grocery shopping, she picked up her work uniforms from the cleaners and then headed home. Up ahead, road signs detoured traffic off the highway where Maxine spotted a "Now Hiring" sign. It was in front of a nursing agency building located in the Webster Groves area. She pulled over to put the number in her cell phone. *God, is this a sign to step out on faith and apply for another job?* Maxine thought as she drove home.

Return Home

When Maxine got home, she was surprised to hear Thelma's voice from upstairs loud and clear.

"You are all I need to get……………. By, yes indeed," Thelma sang over the music.

 Thelma was in Maxine's master bathroom in the Jacuzzi tub blowing bubbles in the air. Maxine was pissed.

"GIRLFRIEND, YOU RECOVERED FAST. GET YOUR ASS UP OUT OF MY TUB. YOU KNOW DAMN WELL YOU COULD HAVE TAKEN A BATH OR SHOWER IN THE OTHER BATHROOM," Maxine yelled.

"Stop being such a bitch. I don't have the cooties, so you have nothing to worry about. What did you bring me back to eat? I drank a whole pot of black coffee to make myself feel a lot better. I also want to say thank you for throwing me the best party of my life! You are my home girl, and no matter what, I'm going to always be around. Thank you," Thelma said blowing bubbles at her.
 "Yeah, yeah, yeah, Thelma. There is no need to thank me for anything that I do for you. You have been around for my life's highs and lows. Only you and my sister can get me to do what I do for you. Now, have your ass out of my tub by the time I put the groceries away."

"Where are all the free pictures we took at the night club, Maxine?"

"The pictures are still in my car because I was dragging your drunk ass into my apartment. Now get your ass out of my tub before I scream, Thelma," Maxine snapped as she exited the bathroom.

Thelma threw up her middle finger so that Maxine could see it. Maxine just smiled and left, closing the bathroom door behind her.

Back At Work

It was a regular busy Monday at work for Maxine. She was preparing a room for a patient being transferred from another floor when her co-worker J.T. walked by.

"J.T., I'm so tired, and I haven't even made it halfway through my shift," Maxine said with a half-smile.

"I feel you, Maxine. I messed up and let this chick come over to my place last night. We ended up going to sleep at about 5 a.m. The bad part about me allowing her to come over is that she ran her mouth about her baby daddy all night. I didn't want to hear all this female's personal business, but I didn't want to look like an asshole just wanting some ass for the night. I just sat and listened to her troubles."

"J.T., it sounds like you had one hell of a night. But keep in mind there's nothing wrong with being a gentleman; sex isn't everything. You're getting up there in age so it's time for you to be settling down with one woman. You don't want to be like some of these patients that get admitted to the hospital sitting all alone," Maxine said laughing.

Maggie, another co-worker, walked by to drop a load of dirty laundry down the chute and overheard Maxine and J.T.'s conversation.

"What's up y'all?" Maggie asked as she stood before her co-workers.

"Nothing much," Maxine said nonchalantly, not wanting to really respond.

Maxine really didn't care for Maggie.

"Hey Maggie, are you done taking care of all of your patients' beds and baths?" J.T. asked as he stood beside her.

Maggie nodded and then walked away.

J.T. noticed Maxine's facial expression once Maggie walked away.

 "What's up with that look?"

"Oh nothing," Maxine said, not wanting to waste time talking about a person she didn't care for.

"Maxine, we are cooler than that. Don't play me off by saying nothing. I want to beware if I need to be when Maggie is around me."

"I just do not like backstabbing bitches. Maggie will grin in your face and run to tell a nurse what you did or not do behind your back. I do not know how she benefits from being so messy."

"You women see shit we men don't pay attention to but stop worrying about the haters. Make your money, and do not be bitter ...with your fine, self." J.T. continued smiling. "I got the message when you suggested I settle down with one woman. I believe that sooner not later that special someone will come my way. I'm claiming it. I'm going to finish making these beds, so I can hide out."

Maxine walked away from J.T. smiling and went to the laundry chart. Maggie was running her mouth at the nurse station not knowing that Maxine was a few steps away hearing her word for word as she spoke.

"If you look down the hallway you will see Maxine and J.T. running their mouths just standing there doing nothing. I needed some help, and neither one of them were willing to lend a helping hand, Ms. Hyson," Maggie said not noticing her co-worker now standing behind her.

This bitch is at least 50 plus years old and acting as though she's 16, Maxine thought. She walked from behind Maggie to in front of her. Maggie gave a fake smile when she saw Maxine in front of her not sure of what she may have overheard.

"Jan, can you page Ricky for me and let him know that I am going to lunch since all my beds are made and patients are taken care of? No one needs my assistance, so I am leaving the floor," Maxine stated, looking directly at Maggie when she spoke to the secretary.

"Sure Maxine, I'll page Ricky for you. Would you mind bringing me back a soda? Any kind will do. I'll have your money when you come back to the floor," Jan said as she answered an incoming call.

"Sure," Maxine said as she 'mean-mugged' Maggie before getting on the elevator.

After catching Maggie in another lie, Maxine decided from that day forward she would just speak to her when spoken to and keep it moving. *I'm allowing this "Auntie" to get my blood boiling,* Maxine thought while riding the elevator down to the cafeteria. After talking to a few of her co-workers from other departments and eating a decent lunch, Maxine was calm enough to go back to work without having an attitude.

When leaving the cafeteria, Maxine saw a position posted on the job board that caught her eye. Once she saw it, Maxine knew she better apply for this job before it was too late. The job that Maxine was going to apply for was in the Emergency department, Monday- Friday with weekends off and a pay increase. *I am going back to the floor to ask Ms. Hyson for a transfer form to fill out right now. I wonder why Thelma didn't tell me about this opening in her department.* Maxine thought.

At the end of her shift, Maxine went to Ms. Hyson's office to get the transfer form required to apply for the Emergency department position. Maxine knew she didn't have any write-ups that would prevent her from applying for the job and getting it.

Ms. Hyson really did not want to lose Maxine as an employee in her department. She was dependable and hard-working but wanted to help her advance in her career. After Maxine filled out the job transfer form and gave it right back to Ms. Hyson, she left the office praying to God that she would get the job. Ms. Hyson signed the transfer form giving her approval for Maxine to apply for the Emergency department position to transfer. Then Ms. Hyson called a friend who was a supervisor in the Emergency department to put in a good word so that Maxine got the patient care tech position. *I hope to get a decent employee replacement once Maxine is gone,* Ms. Hyson thought as she got ready to go and help work with the patients on the Cardia floor.

Transfer

Thanks to Ms. Hyson, Maxine got the job in the Emergency department after just one interview. Thelma was happy to be working with Maxine at first, but then grew jealous when she discovered how smart her best friend was. Maxine was able to make her own blood draw labels without waiting on the secretary to do so. She was also chosen to teach some of the patient care techs how to effectively use the weight scales installed on the hospital beds. Many of the techs didn't know how to operate them. Thelma just could not stand the sight of Maxine, knowing that she was receiving a pay raise for her job knowledge.

Dr. Slone went down to the Emergency department to see how Maxine was maintaining. He peeped in one of the patient's rooms where a nurse told him Maxine was drawing blood.

"Hi Dr. Slone, I'll be out of here in a minute so that you can talk to your patient," Maxine said with a friendly smile.

Dr. Slone didn't respond. He just let the door close and patiently waited in the hallway. Thelma was getting ready to clock out but stalled around to find out why Dr. Slone was in her department. Maxine told Thelma that she was not talking to Dr. Slone much anymore. *If Maxine isn't fucking around with Dr. Slone anymore, then why is he down here looking for her?* Thelma thought. Maxine came out of the patient's room still smiling with Dr. Slone smiling right back.

"You can go in now to see your patient, Dr. Slone," Maxine confirmed, trying to keep the conversation on a professional level.

"No one is around, Maxine, so you don't have to call me doctor. I came down here to see how things were working out for you."

"Things are going well. The days and nights go by so fast with the rotation of patients. I can't believe I've been down here for a month already, Chad."

"Well, I'm glad to see that you have peace. Maybe the next step will be going back to school to get your degree. Since the weekend starts tomorrow how about we do lunch and catch a movie?" he suggested.

Maxine agreed to Dr. Slone's suggestion then cut the conversation short so she could get back to work. It had been five months since their first date, and Dr. Slone planned to really impress Maxine on this date.

Meanwhile Thelma shook her head, feeling betrayed that Maxine was keeping secrets from her. "I have secrets of my own too, Maxine. So ain't no trip if you want to be like that ... fine then," Thelma mumbled to herself before she clocked out to go home.

I'm Impressed

The weekend turned out to be mind-blowing for Maxine. Dr. Slone rented a pearl white SL 550 Mercedes Benz to take Maxine to a winery for a jazz concert. She had never seen a live jazz band perform and looked forward to the entertainment. The two of them sampled different wines and cheeses, had enjoyable conversation, and shared a kiss as they looked over the green pasture.

"I made other plans for us later today if it's okay with you," he said as he gently rubbed Maxine's shoulder.

"There are more plans in store for us today? You have outdone yourself already by bringing me here in that fancy car and showing me a great time, Chad."

Maxine and Dr. Slone enjoyed the live band. Before leaving the winery, Dr. Slone purchased a couple of bottles of wine for Maxine to take home to enjoy. It was a wonderful day as she sat in the passenger seat feeling so relaxed during the drive back to the city. She hummed to the music and let the wind blow through her hair.

"You are a nice-looking woman. How many men have told you that already?" Dr. Slone asked, glancing at her.

She smiled as she saw Dr. Slone looking in her direction. "Not too many men get the chance to tell me how I look. You are not bad on the eyes yourself.

Tell me why you are without a girlfriend, wife, or any children," Maxine asked wanting to know some of Dr. Slone's personal business.

"I put my career before a relationship most of my adult life. When I was in medical school, I almost married a woman who was a nurse. She had an abortion without consulting with me, stating her career was more important. That situation really did something to me, so after that I never took interest in another serious relationship."
Maxine realized she was not the only person in the world who had been through something major.

Dr. Slone made reservations for dinner at Munnion's, an Italian restaurant in the heart of the city. Munnion's was located on the corner of Page and Newstead Avenue. Dr. Slone parked right in front of the Italian restaurant, got out of the car, and walked to the passenger door to help Maxine out of the car. The two walked in the restaurant holding hands and were seated right away. Dr. Slone sat quiet at the table.
"Chad, what is on your mind? I didn't mean to ask questions to upset you, by any means. If you want to end our date, you can take me home now."

Dr. Slone got up from the table and sat beside Maxine.

"Do you mind if I sit next to you, beautiful lady?" he asked.

Maxine leaned over and gave Chad a kiss on the cheek.

"No, I don't mind at all that you're next to me," she said blushing.

Dr. Slone ordered an appetizer for them and a bottle of wine. The waiter returned with two glasses of water and a basket of parmesan crusted garlic bread nuggets.

"That bread smells so good, Chad"

"Why don't you taste the bread instead of looking at it? You are depriving yourself if you do not indulge in it," Dr. Slone teased as he took a second bite of the garlic bread nuggets.

 Once the main course arrived, Maxine reconsidered about eating healthy and enjoyed the eggplant, spaghetti, fried zucchini, and flamingo grilled steak.

"Thank you, Chad, for such a beautiful day."

"Cheers to you, Maxine."

Notice of Change

The Emergency department was like a ghost town. There were only five patients in the waiting room. Most of the time, there were thirty patients or more waiting to be seen. Maxine left the Emergency department to get something to drink since things were slow. She daydreamed as she waited for the elevator to get back to her department. Thelma walked up behind Maxine like a thief in the night.

"Oh girl, I didn't even notice you standing behind me," Maxine said as she looked at her best friend while walking into the elevator.

"I noticed you weren't watching your surroundings. What's on your mind? It looks like you were deep in thought about something or someone. Has anything else transpired from your sons' school situation?" Thelma asked, trying to pick her friend's brain.

"The school issue is over with. Everything is fine with the boys and school. I was just thinking about my date with Chad. He is beginning to grow on me a little bit. We went to this winery over in Alton, Illinois and had an enjoyable time. You and I need to go together when we are both free to chill out for the day," Maxine said with excitement.

Thelma was not thinking about going anyplace with Maxine and wasn't too interested in hearing about her secret relationship with Dr. Slone.

"It's nice to finally hear about you and Dr. Slone – a person you really had no interest in the last time I asked you about him," Thelma said sarcastically.

Thelma walked out of the elevator along with Maxine then took a left turn in the hallway to clock-in. She walked to the cubicle seating area smiling as she grabbed a headset to register Emergency patients. Maxine suddenly noticed that Thelma wasn't wearing the same burgundy patient care tech uniform. *Yeah bitch, get to walking like a chicken with its head cut off while I sit comfortably on my ass for eight hours registering these patients,* Thelma thought as she stared at Maxine with hate in her eyes.

Brittany, one of their co-workers came in and sat beside Thelma giving her a high-five. Brittany put on her headset to work as a unit secretary. Deep in thought, Maxine was observing all this and trying to figure out why Thelma was acting differently towards her.

"Thanks, Thelma, for telling me about this unit secretary position. We are both going to be getting paid to sit, girlfriend," Brittany said as she stored her purse in her desk drawer.

Brittany saw Maxine looking their way, so she spoke and waved.

"Hey Maxine," Brittany said with a friendly smile.

Maxine waved backed and spoke to Brittany before walking away to take care of a patient.

Things were awkward at work between Maxine and Thelma. On a few occasions, Maxine had to restrain herself from choking the hell out of Thelma, because Thelma liked to play mind games. Maxine would get a text message from Thelma to do a task, and then Thelma would lie about sending the message. *I have bills to pay and can't afford to have a criminal record if Thelma and I get into a physical altercation on the job*, Maxine thought working to stay calm. Mad as hell, Maxine thought about the four EKGs ordered on patients that didn't need the procedure done – all completed before clocking out on time to go home.

One Year Later

One year had passed, Maxine had been working a fulltime job as a patient care tech in the Emergency department and a part-time job as a field supervisor assistant with the nursing agency in the Webster Groves area. The hard work had paid off for Maxine, who had saved up enough money to buy a house. Maxine had been packing boxes for weeks and could not wait to move into her new home in a couple of days.

"Momma, here's the mail," Ahmad said as he handed her a stack of envelopes.

"Thank you, son" Maxine said as she reached for the mail before her son headed back outside to play basketball.

 Maxine took a break from packing and poured herself a glass of wine before opening the envelope from the housing department.

Dear Ms. Gamble,

It was brought to our attention that all income was not reported during the time of your stay at Cotton Willow Apartments. Our financial advisor pulled your records based on your social security number and found that you did not report your child support as a part of your income. It has been determined that you owe $7,321.90 to avoid being taken to court.

What the hell? How did they know about my child support money? Maxine thought. She wondered who told her personal business. Maxine called the leasing office about the letter sent from the housing department. Kelly, the office manager, put Maxine on hold after listening to her complaint then came right back to talk.

"Maxine, I believe someone may have made a mistake by sending you that letter from this office. There isn't anything indicating that you owe any back rent, but someone did call the office recently to report you made more income than you claimed to be making. Her name was Thelma Green," Kelly explained as she looked at the sticky note attached to Maxine's leasing file.

"WHAT? THAT BITCH USED TO BE MY BEST FRIEND," Maxine yelled, not believing that Thelma had turned into a spiteful bitch for no reason.

"Sounds like you are surprised a female would cross you, Maxine. When you do better there is always someone in the dark trying to turn on the light to expose you to prove nothing because of their insecurities. Congratulations on becoming a homeowner. I am so very proud of you. I remember the day you moved in with your babies, telling me you are going to be on time paying your rent because you needed a roof over your head. Now look at you today, a grown woman with handsome teenage sons, a nice car, and a house of your own to move into. You go girl! Once you're completely moved out, turn in your keys to the apartment so that I can give you your security deposit right away."

"Thanks for everything you have done for me and my family. Once I get settled, I am going to cook dinner so that you can come over and see my new place," Maxine said with tears in her eyes.

Kelly's compliment meant the world to Maxine. *That low-down, dirty bitch Thelma,* Maxine thought as she finished packing to move.

Last Day on The Job

Maxine was a bit relieved to be getting out of a dead-end job. Being a patient care technician was a great job for someone that was young or going to nursing school, but not a good long-term job for someone in her 50s or late 60s to be retiring from. Taking orders from a nurse young enough to be her child was not Maxine's plan any longer. She happily passed out invitations to her "New Journey in Life" party to a few of her co-workers.

Thelma saw Maxine walking her way as she smirked and waited on an invitation. She had overheard that Maxine was having a party and knew it would be a fun time, because Maxine knew how to entertain and have fun. *I miss my friend. It was wrong of me not to tell Maxine about the unit secretarial position and wrong to call the leasing office on her to just mess with her head, but oh well, she'll forgive me. We'll make up at her party, and things will be back to normal,* Thelma thought.

Maxine smirked back at Thelma because she knew what the spiteful bitch was thinking. "Hey girl," Maxine said as she approached the patient registration desk.

"Hey Maxine! What's up girl?" Brittany asked as she was getting ready to clock out and go home.

"Nothing much Brittany; I'm just glad this is my last day working here. My time has come to move on. I would like for you to help me celebrate if you are off tomorrow night," Maxine said with a smile as Thelma kept her eyes on her.

"Girl yes, I will be there. Thanks for the invite," Brittany responded reading the invitation.

"Well, see you then," Maxine said as she calmly walked away switching her hips from side to side, laughing on the inside.

Pick your face up off the floor, you spiteful bitch, and close your mouth while you are at it. This past year you have been talking behind my back and playing stupid ass mind games. Then you tried to fuck with my money by reporting my extra income to the damn leasing office and the IRS, Maxine thought as she looked at Thelma.

"Thelma, did you get an invitation from Maxine when I was at lunch? I didn't see Maxine give you one," Brittany asked reaching to get her purse out of her desk drawer. Thelma didn't respond because her feelings were really hurt that Maxine didn't invite her to her "New Journey in Life" party.

Celebrate

Maxine was dressed to impress in a sleeveless red Versace dress that Chad gave her as a gift for her new accomplishments. Maxine thought about the good times that she shared with Thelma as she got dress for the party. She wished things had not gone so terribly wrong between them. *What made that bitch Thelma cross me I will never know,* Maxine thought, as she tried to shake what her best buddy had done to her. Chance walked into his mother's bedroom to let her know her sister was waiting on her downstairs. Maxine ran to the bathroom to comb her hair into a ponytail and then rushed downstairs to greet her sister.

"Girl, you are wearing that dress. It is not wearing you. You have really done a lot of decorating around the house since you moved in. Why don't you give me these pillows? They do not match your décor," Eva said as she picked up one of the pillows from the couch admiring it.

"I'm not giving you my pillows that do match my décor. Excuse yourself. You are trying to get something for nothing. Thanks for the compliment about decorating the house. It's been nothing but work since we moved in here. Now come on; let's go.

I'll drive tonight, big sis," Maxine said grabbing her purse off the coffee table.

Since she was going to be out late, Maxine asked Dee-Dee, someone who had watched the boys for years, to 'teenage sit'.

"Hi Ms. Gamble, you and Ms. Eva are looking cute," Dee-Dee said as she read the designer labels they had on.

"Thank you for the compliment, Dee-Dee," Eva said as she tossed her hair over her shoulder and grabbed her large Prada leather handbag.

Maxine let Dee-Dee know where they would be for the night in case of an emergency, then headed out the front door. Eva smiled as she and her sister walked to the new car. Maxine popped the lock to the Cadillac CT4 by pressing the remote so they could get inside.

"Maxine, did you keep the Mustang?" Eva asked as she lit a cigarette.

"No ma'am I didn't keep the Mustang. I traded the Mustang in. You know damn well I can't afford two car note payments at one time. I wanted a new living situation, new employment along with a new car, so the 'ole' bitches wouldn't be able to keep up with me," Maxine chuckled, starting up the car.

"I feel you on that note. You haven't mentioned Thelma lately. Will she be at the party tonight?" Eva asked while popping her fingers to the music.

"I told you a while back that I don't talk to Thelma anymore. Let's talk about something or someone else instead of that low-life bitch," Maxine suggested.

"It's a shame you two can't work whatever it is out."

Being the youngest, Maxine ignored Eva's comment trying not to disrespect her sister as she kept talking about Thelma. Eva was five years Maxine's elder with regrets of not spending enough quality time with her baby sister while away at college.

When Maxine parked in front of the night club, she gave her sister a look of approval as a gentleman helped her out of the car. Maxine strutted in the nightclub with her six-inch heels and long legs looking to see if anybody she knew was in the V.I.P. section she had reserved.

The nightclub was packed from wall to wall. Chad was sitting in the V.I.P section looking for Maxine to walk in any minute. He spotted her within the crowd of people near the bar walking towards him.

"Hey Doc," Eva said as she popped her fingers to the music dancing on the side of him.

"What's up, Eva?" Dr. Slone asked, happy to see her.

Eva leaned over to whisper in Maxine's ear.

"When did you teach Dr. Slone how to talk slang? He's not from the hood, is he?"

Maxine laughed.

"Stop it, Eva. I keep telling you Chad is just as hip to the game as we are. Don't get it twisted because he's a doctor," Maxine replied.

"So, are you and Chad dating now?" Eva asked, being nosey.

"Chad and I aren't dating; we're just 'kicking it'. Enjoy the party, why don't you. You're full of damn questions tonight," Maxine said, dancing by the table as she greeted more of her invited guests that had just arrived.

"Last question: are y'all fucking?"

"Mind your business, big sis," Maxine warned before walking away to the dance floor.

Wanting to get the party started, Maxine danced by herself since no one was out on the dance floor. The DJ was jamming, playing all the latest #1 hits. Eva had to encourage Chad to get on the dance floor with Maxine before some random dude walked up on her. Not having much rhythm, Chad walked out on the dance floor next to Maxine. All Maxine could do was laugh at Chad moving off beat to the music.

"Give me your hands, Chad," Maxine said, still laughing at him.

She pumped his hands up in the air.

"Wave your hands in the air! Wave them like you just don't give a care!" Maxine shouted over the music.

The liquor Chad drank before Maxine arrived started having a major effect on him. His tall physique stood over Maxine's slender body as she rocked her hips to the music. Just as she was getting into the grove, Oliver Boyd and his male friends walked in. *Oh shit! Who would have thought I would ever bump into my babies' daddy in the club? He's going to be tripping if he sees me with Chad and threaten not to pay his child support,* Maxine thought.

Eva came to the rescue by cutting in to dance with Chad so that her sister could briefly talk to Oliver.

"I'm going to show the Doc how to get down," Eva said joking around with her sister.

Maxine stepped aside so that Eva could take over dancing with Chad. Oliver was still mesmerized by Maxine's beauty as she walked his way. He was surprised that she was even in a nightclub knowing that she wasn't the clubbing type. Nevertheless, but he was happy to see her.

There was an age difference between Oliver and Maxine, so some things could not be overlooked. She hadn't matured to his standards back then. Now that Maxine was an adult, she had her shit together. Oliver entertained the thought of an on-and-off fling, but he knew Maxine wouldn't go for any shit like that. "What's up Maxine? What are you doing in the night club? Who's watching our sons?" Oliver asked, trying to act like a full-time parent.

"Our sons are older now, so I can go out from time to time without any worries," Maxine replied.

She was getting ready to walk away after saying hello and goodbye, but Oliver excused himself first. He spotted his significant other walking into the night club. Maxine wasn't bothered by Oliver being with a woman. The timing of the female greeting Oliver could not have been better so that Maxine could return to her male companion. Dancing her way back across the dance floor, Maxine was enjoying herself.

She tapped Eva on the shoulder so that she could relieve her feet from the five-inch heels that she was dancing in. Eva gave Maxine a wink, grateful that Maxine had come back to dance with Chad. She had contemplated taking her heels off to dance barefoot.

"Everybody, throw your hands up if you're having a good time!" the DJ yelled.

Maxine and Chad threw their hands up in the air, smiling at each other. Chad hadn't had that much fun in a nightclub since his freshman year in college.

Oliver looked out on the dance floor and saw Maxine wrapped up in Chad's arms as they slow danced. His female friend was talking her head off as Oliver focused on Maxine and her male companion. Then Chad noticed the man walking their way, looking like a mad man. He wondered where the man was going until Oliver stopped right in front of them.

"Maxine, who the fuck is this chump you all wrapped up with?" Oliver asked, making himself look like he had some type of mental problem.

Maxine could not believe that Oliver was acting like a jealous boyfriend. It had been years since they had been in a relationship.

"Go back to where you came from, Oliver. Don't start some shit you can't get out of," Maxine warned while grabbing Chad's arm to walk away.

Oliver pushed Chad to start a fight. Chad turned around looking like a mad man and punched Oliver in the face, knocking him out.

"NO CHAD!" Maxine yelled.

Eva tried to keep the fight from escalating, but it was too late. Oliver's male friends came rushing towards the dance floor, but security blocked their path. The party was officially over. Fights were breaking out all over the nightclub for unknown reasons. Chad escorted Maxine and Eva safely to their car to make sure they were secure and apologized for ruining their night out.

Tonight, Is the Night

Maxine drove home listening to Eva talk about the fight between Oliver and Chad non-stop. She pulled up in front of her house and put her car in park so that Eva could get out giving her peace and quiet.

"Give Dee-Dee this money for keeping an eye on the boys. I need you to stay at my house until I come back in a few hours, Eva. I'm going over to Chad's house to talk for a while and have a few drinks," Maxine said, smiling at her sister.

"Keep your money, Maxine. I paid Dee-Dee before we left the house tonight. Be careful, and text me when you get to Doc's place so I know you made it there safely," Eva said smiling back at Maxine. The sisters hugged one another before Eva got out of the car.

As Maxine drove to Chad's house she hoped for the best. It had been a long time since Maxine allowed a man to get physically close to her. When Maxine pulled up in front of Chad's home, she was second guessing if she really was ready for whatever may happen once she went inside. Chad had jazz playing low with the lights dimmed when he greeted Maxine at the door. He gently grabbed Maxine by the hand and kissed it softly. Chad was glad that Maxine had accepted his invitation.

"Welcome to my home," Chad said as he closed the front door behind her.

The click from Maxine's shoes on the hardwood floor made Chad's dick rock hard. He watched her shapely legs as she walked.

"Come sit next to me, Chad. I won't bite you," Maxine said seductively.

Chad grabbed a glass of wine from the coffee table handing it to Maxine as he sat beside her. He took a sip of wine then sat the glass back down on the table.

"Maxine, I am sorry about tonight. The incident made me truly come out of my character."

"There is no need for an apology. The man you knocked out is my sons' father. I can't explain what made him react the way he did, but I can assure you that there's nothing between us."

Chad rubbed Maxine's leg gently. She blushed from the man's touch. After seeing how Chad put his hands on Oliver, she knew she wasn't going to be buying batteries for a while if she ever gave him a chance to come and get it. *He is educated, established, stable, has his own home, has never been married, and does not have any baby mommas to deal with – my kind of man,* Maxine thought.

"I want you to kiss me, Chad," she said in such a seductive tone, she turned herself on.

Chad kissed Maxine with his soft, fat juicy lips as she asked him to do. When he slowly rubbed his fingertips across her collar bone, Maxine felt chills run down her spine.

The heat of Chad's warm breath went across her earlobe when he spoke.

"Please join me in the bedroom," he said.

Maxine didn't want to move away from the couch. She was a bit intoxicated but was aware of what she was about to do. She laced her tongue with Chad's as she finished unbuttoning his shirt to touch his masculine chest. He unzipped the back of Maxine's dress and let it fall to her waist, exposing her full, round breasts.

"Let me stand up so I can step out of my dress," she said as she gave him another kiss on the lips.

Chad stood to his feet to finish undressing himself as he looked down closely at Maxine's voluptuous body. She stepped out of her dress, leaving on nothing but her lace thong and heels. She wasn't ashamed of her few stretch marks or the little pudgy stomach she had from giving birth to three babies.

Chad guided Maxine down to the bear skin rug in front of the fireplace. He was very well-endowed. Chad began fingering Maxine's clitoris, getting it nice and wet as they kissed one another. Maxine opened the condom that she carried in her clutch purse and put it on Chad's shaft. Then she straddled him as he cupped her breasts with his strong hands. *Damn, it*

feels so good to be touched by a man that's in control,
Maxine thought as she continued to ride his dick.
Chad wanted to be in control, so he gently flipped
Maxine over onto the rug and began to give strong,
slow strokes as he went in and out of her.

"Am I hurting you?"

"No, you're not hurting me. I want you to hurt this
black cat and make it meow. I love sexual
punishment," Maxine said as she moaned.

Talk To Me

Maxine walked into her house Monday morning as quiet as a mouse to see Eva cooking breakfast.

"Good morning, Ms. *Thang*. I'm glad you decided to come home," Eva joked.

"Yeah, it was time to come back to where I live. Thanks for staying the rest of the weekend with the boys. I really needed that little getaway," Maxine said with a huge smile plastered on her face.

Tyson, Ahmad, Myron, and Chance ran downstairs and grabbed their lunch bags and breakfast sandwiches before walking out of the house.

"Good morning, Momma" the boys said, hugging Maxine.

"Hey! Good morning,"

"Hi, Auntie Maxine. You look nice in that dress, but it's on inside out. Bye, Momma! Have a good day at work," Tyson shouted, walking out the door behind his cousins.

"What?" Maxine shouted, now realizing she put her clothes on the wrong way before leaving Chad's house. Eva looked out of the window to watch the boys get on the school bus.

Once Eva looked through the window and saw the boys get on the school bus safely, she began asking questions.

"Talk to me, girl, and tell me what in the world you've been doing with the doctor since you dropped me off Saturday night. Your dress is on inside out, so I know for sure the garment has been off your body" Eva said with a devilish grin.

"Well, Chad and I had a few drinks by the fireplace to get to know each other a little better," Maxine said, stalling with the story.

Eva chewed her food and then gave her baby sister a serious look knowing that she was leaving out the best part of the story.

"You and I know damn well you didn't go over to Doc's house late Saturday night to sit by no damn fireplace getting to know each other better. Start talking and don't leave any of the sexual parts out."

Maxine laughed.

"Ok, ok, ok... after seeing how Chad stood his ground with Oliver, I desired to be with him sexually. When Chad invited me over, I sat in my car before going in his house thinking this was an all or nothing situation. When I walked inside the house, music was playing, the lights were dimmed, and the fireplace was burning. One thing led to another, and the rest I let Chad handle sexually until he left for work this

140

morning. That's when I decided to come home," Maxine said smiling.

"Damn…….. Maxine! So, this means you don't have to buy any batteries for a while, huh? Mr. Mix is going to be stored away in the closet?" Eva asked laughing her ass off.

"Damn right! Dr. Chad Slone has a dick the size of an elephant's trunk. It's long and thick how I like it. I am going to put that *thang* to good use while it's available for *ya* girl. It is not that often that a man is blessed with a 'pipe fitting' and knows how to really use it," Maxine said, giving her sister a high-five before walking out of the kitchen.

Enjoying the New Job

Maxine was really enjoying her new job at the nursing agency working full-time as a field assistant supervisor. She had to personally check on the employees to make sure they were at work on time.

Some clients would call and say that the employee told them they would be off, and their replacement would fill in when the office wasn't aware of the arrangements. Then there were cases where employees who didn't show up for work were having the client sign their timesheet in advance as though they worked that day to be paid for it.

One day someone is going to come up with a brilliant idea where you have to call from the client's home to clock-in. It will identify your location and the time to confirm you're on the job and on time, Maxine thought as she looked at the timesheets she had collected to turn in for payroll. Maxine walked into her supervisor's office with a smile as she placed the stack of timesheets on her desk.

"Maxine, can you visit Mrs. Fee-Fee Buntals to see what the problem is over there? Her daughter called saying an employee was sent to the store to buy some groceries but didn't give the client a receipt when they returned. The daughter is speculating that the employee is stealing from her mother,"

Charmaine said as she searched on the computer screen to find a more suitable caregiver.

Charmaine was the nursing office manager/client access specialist that covered most of the problems between clients and employees. Knowing how knowledgeable Maxine was, Charmaine asked her to manage the small issues that didn't involve a lot of paperwork.

Back out of the office, Maxine was now in route to Mrs. Buntals' home. When Maxine pulled up at the client's house, the employee, Minnie, was just arriving to work twenty minutes late. Minnie tried to keep her composure when she saw Maxine getting out of the car.

"Hi, Ms. Maxine," Minnie said, walking toward the client's house as though she had just come back from running an errand for the client.

Maxine greeted Minnie and felt that the energy was off as they walked together towards Mrs. Buntals' house. Once inside, Maxine asked Minnie to join her in the living room to sit with the family.

"Mrs. Buntals, my name is Maxine Gamble. I am one of the nursing agency's field supervisors. I'm here to address the issue with the misuse of your credit card," she said.

Minnie felt extremely uncomfortable. She knew she was in trouble when Carlie, Mrs. Buntals' daughter, handed a copy of the credit card statement to Maxine. Carlie was terribly upset after discovering Minnie had stolen from her mom by purchasing items for herself.

"I would like to press charges against Minnie because my mother trusted her. There is no telling what else she's been stealing unbeknownst to my mother and me," Carlie said as though her feelings were truly hurt.

Carlie Buntals really did not care about the funds spent on her mother's credit card. She just wanted to have something to bitch about when she saw her girlfriends at their next Tuesday gathering. They usually met up to play card games like Bridge and Mahjong every Tuesday night.

"Ma'am, I understand your frustration. That's why I am here to handle the problem. The total of the bill was $27.83. The company will reimburse your mother for the bill and give her two days of free service for her trouble," Maxine said, trying to smooth things over.

Minnie felt relieved that Maxine was talking Mrs. Buntals' daughter out of calling the police to press charges. She figured that, at most, the cost of what she had charged on the credit card was going to be deducted from her paycheck; and she would be transferred to another client. Maxine reached inside her briefcase and handed Minnie a form to sign. It was a notice of termination.

"Minnie, can you sign this form before you leave, please? It's indicating that you are aware that your paycheck will be held as reimbursement to the nursing agency for the inconvenience of stealing from the client," Maxine said with a stern look on her face.

Mrs. Buntals' doorbell rang during the meeting. Carlie excused herself to answer the door. Right on time, the employee that Charmaine scheduled to meet Maxine at Mrs. Buntals' house had arrived.

"Hello, Ms. Maxine," Roxanna said as she entered the room.

"Hi, Roxanna! I am glad you were available to work today. Mrs. Buntals, this will be Minnie's replacement. You will be pleased to have her working for you. She is familiar with Yiddish, your native language," Maxine said with a smile.

"Roxanna, you're so tall and pretty! You look as strong as an ox," Mrs. Buntals said, complimenting and insulting her at the same time.

Lord, have mercy, was all Maxine could think as she listened to Mrs. Buntals talking and Roxanna saying yes ma'am repeatedly. Minnie was asked to leave the premises after signing the document. Then Maxine asked Mrs. Buntals to sign a nondisclosure agreement form stating that she wouldn't file any charges against the employee or the nursing agency. Maxine was pleased to have handled Mrs. Buntals' issues without Charmaine's assistance.

"Thank you all for your time. If you have any problems in the future, please do not hesitate to call. Here is my business card," Maxine said as she stood up to leave.
Mrs. Buntals thanked Maxine, and Carlie walked her to the door thanking her for taking care of the problem. As Maxine got in her car, she realized that she really liked her job. *Now it's time to go eat with my boo,* Maxine thought thinking about her man. Maxine was fifteen minutes away from where she was to meet her boyfriend. Chad smiled when he saw Maxine walk into the café.

 "Hey baby. How is your day going so far?" she asked as she kissed Chad's cheek.

"*Wasss* up babe. I can't complain. I just have the normal patient load I'm used to having." He paused and smiled at her. "Enough talking about me. How's your day going?"

"Well, this employee in her late 40s used this client's credit card to buy some steamed vegetables and other items from the grocery store. Best part is, she thought she was going to get away with it. The client's daughter wanted to file a police report against the employee after discovering what was done. That report would have involved the company's name and reputation.

Charmaine told me to terminate the employee, reimburse the client for the charges on her credit card, and offer two free days of services," Maxine explained as she leaned in closer. "Then there's another stupid story that I must tell you before I forget. One of our part-time registered nurses also works as a head nurse at a nursing home full-time. Apparently, word got back to our corporate office that she was teaching a certified nurse's assistant class at the nursing home. She was teaching it after business hours to fulfill clinical hours but didn't advise the administration.

Turns out this nurse is going to lose her nursing license, because one of the students claims she got hurt while doing her clinical hours!" Maxine held her head while eating her salad.

"What a liability that situation was. That's a shame. Well, enough talk about outside issues that don't pertain to us. Let's toast to you for getting out of your comfort zone and doing different things in life," Chad said, congratulating his woman.

Maxine and Chad clicked their water glasses as he commended her on her new accomplishments.

Opportunity To Make More Money

Maxine usually volunteered to work overtime for the weekend when an employee called off work at the last minute. Since Maxine was a patient care technician at her old job, Charmaine recommended that she test to become a certified nurse assistant. This would benefit Maxine and the company; she could work in the field when needed on any assignment.

Maxine made an appointment with the nursing instructor Charmaine connected her with, and she passed the test with excellence. Maxine was grateful for the pay increase and the weekends off to spend time with her family. Being a team player, she was eager to assist when Charmaine called her to work the private duty assignment at the last minute.

Maxine parked her car in front of the client's mansion and stared at the stunning English Tudor estate and well-manicured lawn. *Damn, I wonder how much it takes to keep that house functional,* Maxine thought as she got out of her car. She pressed the doorbell and immediately someone opened the door. A tall woman with a brown skin complexion and shoulder-length, sandy brown hair with frosted tips opened the door smiling.

"Hi, you must be Maxine. I'm Yandy; it's nice to meet you," she said, reaching out to shake Maxine's hand.

Yandy stepped aside so that Maxine could walk into the house. Maxine was amazed to see how the rich and famous really lived in the Frontenac area of Missouri.

"This is a really nice home," Maxine said as she looked around.

Yandy walked down the hallway to the laundry room rocking her hips from side to side in her skin-tight True Religion blue jeans and low-cut Fendi t-shirt. "Thanks for the compliment, Maxine. People always say how nice the house looks when they see it for the first time. Hang your sweater up in this closet here if you want. You can put your purse in that cabinet over there to the right. If you can't reach the handle to the cabinet, there's a step stool over to the right in the corner," Yandy said as she pointed toward the cherry wood cabinets in the laundry room.

Maxine was just as tall as Yandy so she simply walked over to the cabinet and stored away her purse. She kept her sweater in hand. The central air was freezing cold inside the house. She followed Yandy as they walked into the master bedroom to be introduced to Mrs. Deere.

"Momma, meet ah... What's your name again?" Yandy asked as though she had forgotten Maxine's name.

"My name is Maxine Gamble. I'm pleased to meet you, Mrs. Deere, even though I can't see you from inside your closet," Maxine said smiling as she waited for the client to appear.

Mrs. Deere walked out of her closet, and Maxine was speechless when she laid eyes on the old Caucasian woman in her late eighties. Mrs. Deere was 5'4" and weighed about 230 pounds. She had snow white hair and a pale complexion.

"Nice to meet you, Maxine, and please call me Pearl. Make yourself at home. I'm looking for my pink button-down shirt that I wear almost every day. Yandy, will you show Maxine around? Help yourself to the refreshments in the kitchen. I'll call you if I need something, sweetheart" she said before going back into the walk-in closet.

Yandy walked out of the master bedroom with Maxine following right behind her. Maxine assumed that Yandy was adopted being that she was African American and addressing Mrs. Deere as her mother.

The kitchen was massive, the size of a studio apartment. Maxine admired its white furniture, stainless steel appliances, marble floors and granite countertops.

"These are Momma's medications. Give her the next set of meds at 7 p.m. after she eats dinner. Normally, dinner time is at 6 p.m. for her, but you can ask Momma when she's ready to eat. After assisting Momma with the meds, put the few dishes in the dishwasher and sweep and mop the floor before you leave. Don't do any major cleaning. The housekeeping staff is here five days a week. When you're done with all your duties, you can watch cable television in the den over there until it's time for you to go home. The television remote is on the bookshelf to the left," Yandy explained as she sat on one of the bar stools to take off her house shoes and put on her Gucci leather sandals.

"Can I ask you a question?" Maxine asked trying not to be too nosey.

Yandy was fastening her sandal as Maxine talked.

"Sure, go ahead and ask your question, Maxine. I thought I covered everything you needed to know."

"I'm not trying to be disrespectful by no means Yandy, but how old was Mrs. Deere when she adopted you? She's rather up in age."

"Pearl ain't my momma. It's just something I have been calling her since I've been working here," Yandy said laughing.

Instantly Maxine had taken a disliking for Yandy, right then and there.

"So how long have you been working for the nursing agency, Yandy? I haven't seen you at any of the mandatory staff meetings."

"I don't work for the nursing agency. My biological mother and I work for Pearl on our own. The nursing agency you work for has their employees working around us. Are you an aide or a C.N.A.?" Yandy asked, now having questions of her own.

"I'm a field supervisor and a certified nurse assistant," Maxine said with no hesitation.

"That's good. You're a well-rounded employee. Well, it was nice meeting you. My mother will be relieving you tonight. Her name is Holly."

Yandy pulled up her blue jeans to cover her fat ass before grabbing her large leather Gucci purse from the laundry room then waved bye to Maxine. Yandy was parked in the six-car garage. Maxine could feel the bass from Yandy's radio system inside of the house as she slowly drove her car out of the garage. Maxine tried to hide as she looked out of the window to see what kind of car Yandy was driving. Yandy tooted her horn when she spotted Maxine. She was driving a black, two-door Mercedes with tinted windows.

Maxine couldn't believe a grown ass woman like Yandy was calling a person she worked for her mother and that her biological mother worked there too. *I can't wait to hear how Yandy's mother is going to address Mrs. Deere when she arrives,* Maxine thought as she went to take care of the client.

Mrs. Deere was sitting on her bed when Maxine entered the bedroom with a glass of ice-cold lemon-flavored tea. Maxine decided to hang out a while to keep Mrs. Deere company. She and Mrs. Deere had a great conversation about life. In that short amount of time, Mrs. Deere grew fond of Maxine being so attentive toward her.

"So, Maxine, I know you work Monday through Friday in the office mostly. Would you consider working some weekends here?" Mrs. Deere asked, hoping the answer would be yes.

"If you're in a bind and really need someone to work some weekends, I can come out sometimes," Maxine replied as she relaxed in the huge, comfortable recliner beside the bed.

Maxine looked at the clock and excused herself to make sure everything was done by the time Yandy's mother arrived. Just as Maxine finished mopping the floor, Holly came walking into the house. Yandy was the spitting image of her mother, who was tall and slender with a nice shapely body. Holly had a short haircut and was dressed in a Nike jogging suit with matching tennis shoes. Maxine walked over to shake Holly's hand and greet her. Holly walked past Maxine as though she wasn't even there and went straight to Mrs. Deere's bedroom. *Did this bitch just walk past me as though I do not exist?* Maxine thought.

Maxine went to get her purse so that she could say goodbye to Mrs. Deere and leave quickly to avoid Holly.

"Pearl, it was a pleasure meeting you, and I wish you well," Maxine said not looking in Holly's direction.

"It's a joy to have met you as well. Please come over here and give me a hug before you go. I really hope to see you again."

Maxine could see the jealousy in Holly's eyes. Surprisingly Holly didn't address Mrs. Deere as her "momma" like her daughter did when she greeted her boss.

Saturday Night

By the time Maxine made it home, all she wanted to do was take a bath, get under a blanket, and sleep. Chad was out of town at a business convention, and the boys were with their father for the weekend. Maxine ended up watching television and eating popcorn after taking a long hot bath. Just as she got relaxed, her telephone began to ring. It was Eva her sister calling.

"Can Tyson come over? I have a date," Eva said with her fingers crossed hoping her sister wouldn't mind babysitting her nephew at the last minute.

"The boys are not home, but Tyson is welcome to visit with his auntie. Who do you have a date with Eva?"

"The lucky man is one of Doc's colleagues!"

"What's his name the guy you have a date with? Stop beating around the bush," Maxine demanded, getting impatient with her sister.

"Dr. Gerald Fitz," Eva answered while ordering food for Tyson at the drive-thru restaurant.

"Oh, he seems like a nice guy. I ran into him a couple of times at Chad's house, but I never really sat down to have a deep conversation with him."

"Well, let's change the subject because son is in the backseat 'ear hustling'. I will be at your house in about 15 minutes. Would you like a burger or something while I'm getting Tyson something to eat?"

"No thanks sis, I ate already. Just tell Tyson to let himself in when he gets here. I'll go downstairs and unlock the door. Be safe and enjoy your date with Dr. Fitz. Don't forget to text me once you get to your destination."

"I won't forget to text you, sis. Thanks again for letting Tyson come over. I love you."
"I love you too, Evie Eve."

Tyson sat in the backseat mad as his mother drove to his aunt's house. He really didn't want to spend the night knowing his cousins weren't home to play video games with. As Maxine finished watching her favorite sitcom, she got out of bed to microwave some more popcorn and unlock the door. Tyson walked into the house as soon as Maxine unlocked the front door.

"What's up auntie?"

"Hey Ty! Would you like some popcorn?" Maxine asked, handing the bowl of popcorn to her nephew.

"No thanks, auntie; I'm full. I just had a burger and fries. All I want to do is play video games."

"Be my guest, Ty. Everything is hooked up in Ahmad's bedroom," Maxine said, moving aside as her nephew went up the steps.

Crazy Experience

On Sunday morning Maxine cooked breakfast then rushed Ty to eat and get dressed so they wouldn't be late for church. It had been a long time since Maxine had stepped foot inside her parents' church. It felt strange for Maxine to hear the voice of a man she had been trying to reason with for so long. Ironically, her father's sermon was on forgiveness. Pastor had aged quite a bit. He was now wearing his hair cut low and no longer wearing facial hair. He had a few wrinkles around his jawline.

"Let the church say amen," Pastor said as he prayed with his church members.

Eva was sitting beside her mother, who still looked the same as Maxine remembered. Phylencia's hair hung down her back with ringlets in the front. Conservatively dressed in a knee-length black dress and a wide-brimmed red hat, Phylencia represented her First Lady position sitting in the front row with a smile.

"Hi, Momma," Maxine whispered, kissing her mother on the cheek.

"Hey baby! This is a surprise," Phylencia exclaimed quietly, happy to see her youngest daughter.

Phylencia had not seen Maxine in years. Pastor had forced his wife to break off all communication with Maxine when she moved out of the house years ago with their grandchildren. He was angry that Maxine refused to lie and say Oliver raped her, the first time she got pregnant. Pastor had a reputation to maintain, and Maxine ruined it when she got pregnant two more times by Oliver without being married.

Pastor spotted Maxine in the congregation. His youngest daughter as she gave her father a friendly smile during the sermon, but Pastor tried to avoid looking at Maxine because he hadn't forgiven her. Phylencia knew that Pastor was avoiding Maxine, so she tried to make light of things for her daughter's sake by hugging her.

"Your father loves you, Maxine; do not let him get you down. He is an old, stubborn man, and his pride is in the way. Where are my grandsons? I know they are growing like weeds. Tyson, come over here and give Nana some sugar, baby," Phylencia said as she leaned over toward her grandson.

Tyson quickly leaned over and hugged his grandmother then ran to his granddaddy's office to get a few dollars.

"Momma, the boys are growing like weeds. They're with their father. Oliver didn't keep his promise to marry me, but he has always taken care of his children. I know Daddy is still upset to this day, but how long is he going to be mad with the decision that I made years ago? I call the house, and he hangs up on me. I've mailed letters expressing my love for you both and apologizing for the shame that I've caused the family with no reply. Are you cooking Sunday dinner? Maybe I can just stop by and talk to Daddy after we eat. I don't want to cause a scene here," Maxine suggested with tears in her eyes.

"Honey, we are going to someone's church anniversary. Then we're going to pray with some of our members that are in a nursing home," Phylencia said, making up excuses to keep Maxine away as her husband told her to do.

Pastor had beat Phylencia over the years every time she would speak Maxine's name. People who saw Phylencia and her husband together doing their good work in the church envied their relationship. Pastor Gamble had been a devil behind closed doors since the day Maxine moved out of the house. Back then, he had a congregation of 1,300 members and it dropped drastically to about 220 members. With the paycheck being low due to membership and not being able to take care of spending habits, Pastor blamed Maxine. Pastor and Phylencia rebuilt their relationships with most of the members that left, but he still wasn't forgiving toward his daughter.

Eva was heartbroken as she listened to her mother make up excuses to keep Maxine from confronting their father. She recalled being 21, a senior in college, and being forced to marry a man she didn't love at the demands of Pastor because she was pregnant. It was a very abusive marriage. Eva felt like she was stuck in the marriage just to save her father's reputation. After being called to the hospital by the police and fearing that Eva and her unborn child were not going to make it, Pastor honored his daughter's wish for a divorce.

Maxine felt rejected by her mother, so she ended the conversation.

"Momma, tell Daddy I love him no matter how he feels about me," she said before leaving the church.

After Church

Ralphie's Buffet had a line coming out of the door when Maxine pulled into the parking lot. Eva and Tyson were already seated at the table with drinks waiting on Maxine to come so they could eat. Eva gave her sister a pep talk once she had arrived trying to cheer her up.

"Maxine, don't worry about things that are out of your control. Momma and Daddy taught us that. Let things work themselves out. I know that it's been years since Momma and Daddy have been in communication with you but if it's meant to be, it will be. You've been obedient. Daddy just might need you one day," she said.

Maxine nodded, agreeing with Eva.

After lunch Maxine decided to ask Eva about her date with Dr. Fitz but was interrupted by a text message before Eva could respond. ***Meet me outside so I can give you your child support money,*** the text message read.

"Hold that thought, Eva. My babies' daddy is getting ready to drop the boys off. I'll be right back," Maxine said as she got up from the table.

Maxine walked out of the restaurant and spotted Oliver pulling up with a random woman in his passenger seat. She decided to show her babies' daddy how to act when you see your ex has moved on. Maxine spoke to Oliver's woman as the boys got out of the car.

"I'll be right back. I need to talk to Maxine alone," Oliver said to his girlfriend as he got out of the car to follow his baby momma into the restaurant.

"Maxine, here is your money order payment for the boys' child support; and let me tell you something. I suggest that you not have any strange men around my sons. Chance was telling me that you have been staying out late with that asshole I got into it with at the club," he said wanting his baby momma to validate what he was thinking and not what he was told by his son.

Maxine took a step back to look at Oliver like he was crazy.

"Oliver, your woman is in the car. How dare you tell me what I better not be doing around our sons? You had your turn in a relationship with me. Since you moved on years ago and now your fucking spot has been filled, don't be mad. I suggest you get in your car and go," Maxine said, as she walked away from the father of her children.

Eva noticed that Maxine looked upset when she got back to the table. "Are you ok?"

"Yeah, I am fine. Oliver is still acting crazy about that
night he and Chad got into it at the night club. Oliver
doesn't want me to be involved with anyone, but he
can fuck every woman that he meets in the streets,"
Maxine said, pissed off.

Eva just shook her head. After the boys ate ice cream
for dessert, they went home. Later that evening, Eva
showed up at Maxine's house to finish their
conversation from the restaurant. Eva couldn't wait
to tell her sister about her strange date with Dr. Fitz.
Maxine grabbed a bottle of wine from the kitchen
while Eva made herself at home, lying comfortably on
the couch. Maxine entered the living room
energetically ready to hear how the date went with
Chad's friend.

"Would you like a half or full glass of wine, Eva?"

"Pour me a full glass please, sis."

Maxine handed her sister a full glass of wine. Eva
took a deep breath before she began to tell the story.

"Well, come to find out, Dr. Fitz is newly divorced and
now I kind of understand why," Eva said as she
frowned up just thinking about the doctor.

"What's the reason Dr. Fitz is single to mingle? A
dinner date couldn't have been that bad. Damn"

"The dinner date was something to never forget;
trust me when I tell you. Ok, so during dinner at that

elegant restaurant in the Creve Coeur area, I thought I smelled a foul odor a few times. It smelled like someone had passed gas. I even smelled it before we sat down, when he held my chair out for me. I know for a fact Dr. Fitz did let one loose or two or three, because the smell came from his direction three damn times, sis!"

Maxine busted out laughing, not believing Dr. Fitz's rudeness.

"After dinner we went to a bar to have drinks and dance, but his moves on the dance floor didn't impress me. Then he suggested we chill out at his apartment, so we went there, and Dr. Fitz had boxes everywhere. We could barely get into his bedroom to relax."

"Please don't tell me you gave him some ass on the first date. Momma taught us better than that."

"Ah, I *was...* going to give Dr. Fitz some pussy on the first date yes... ma'am. We are grown ass people. Shit, stop judging me and let me finish telling you the story. The bedroom furniture was in place, so I laid across the bed and he began to kiss me down below as he undressed me. Then he got undressed and everything was pleasing to my eyes, including the size of him. He put on a condom and got in between my legs and was about to put himself inside of me when my fingertips ran across something unusual," Eva said, laughing as she recounted the experience.

"What was the issue? Please tell me!"

"Girl, Dr. Fitz's ass crack. There was a lump there in between; and he has a turtle dick," Eva replied with a straight face.

"Wait a minute, Eva! You are telling me he had a lump of shit in the crack of his ass and he's not even circumcised?"

"Yes, sis. That fine, well-spoken, educated man does not know how to properly wipe his ass. I felt small little balls of shit paper in his crack and everything, girl. I was trying to become a 'retainer girlfriend' like you are with Chad, but I'm going to have to pass on that one. All money ain't good money. You must know how to properly wipe your butt crack to deal with me. Also, to have a dick of decent size with all that extra skin, I must say no way. That fool had the nerve to ask if I give head. I told him yes, I do, but not to turtle dick people. I'm moving on to this other man I've been seeing off and on for about a month. His name is Bobby," Eva said as she took another sip from her glass.

"Finish off that bottle of wine. You need it 'sista' after that traumatizing experience. I would have cussed Dr. Fitz's ass out so bad that he wouldn't want to ever see me again. Are your hands clean? I touched both of them," Maxine said laughing.

"Very funny, Maxine. Ha ha," her sister replied.

Monday Morning Rush

Maxine walked in the office of the nursing agency in a good mood. She sat at her desk looking over her report and the list of employees she had to check up on for the day.

"Maxine, can you come to my office please for a moment?" Charmaine asked as she sat down at her desk.

Charmaine's request made Maxine nervous. She wondered why she was having a private meeting with the boss.

"Close the door behind you,"

She closed the door and took a seat.

"Is everything okay, Charmaine?"

"Everything is fine. I wanted to let you know that Mrs. Pearl Deere was really impressed with you. She wants to pay the nursing agency to cancel her contract with us if you are willing to come and work for her."

"I don't quite understand what you're saying. Please know I didn't suggest that I work for Mrs. Deere on my own. I love my job here," Maxine said, letting her supervisor know that she wasn't trying to do anything underhandedly.

Charmaine liked Maxine's honesty.

"I understand you're not trying to do anything wrong, Maxine. This is a job opportunity not too many people get. Mrs. Deere is the owner of Deere Noosa's," Charmaine said as her eyes widened to excite Maxine.

The name didn't ring a bell for Maxine, and Charmaine could tell.

"Okay, have you ever gone to a vending machine to buy snacks?"

"Yes ma'am. I have many times."

"Well, Mrs. Deere and her husband are the people who invented and own the patent to the part that turns and releases the snacks after you insert your money. Mr. and Mrs. Deere are billionaires. Between me and you, I say go work for the lady. You can get another job as a C.N.A. any time to work anywhere."

The wheels in Maxine's head began turning. She stood up shaking Charmaine's hand and walked out of the office, really thinking of how beneficial this job offer could be with the Deeres.

Wednesday

Charmaine scheduled Maxine to work that Wednesday, knowing Mrs. Deere needed someone to work for her that day. It gave Maxine a chance to make a final decision regarding the job with the Deere family. When she arrived at Mrs. Deere's estate, Maxine was on guard. She was about to press the doorbell when Yandy opened the door.
"Hi Maxine, I was about to go and get the mail" she said.

Maxine spoke with Yandy offering to go get the mail since she was already standing on the porch. She walked down the long driveway to the mailbox, happy to get a quick 10-minute walk in. Maxine grabbed the stack of envelopes and couldn't believe it was just a day's worth of mail. She wasn't trying to purposely read the Deere's mail, but she spotted the amount of one of the utility bills through the thin paper envelope. *Ain't this about a bitch! The electric bill is $114.00 for an estate. You got to be kidding me,* Maxine thought as she walked back up the driveway. She walked into the estate and put the mail on the table in the foyer while analyzing Yandy's attire. *This woman is too damn comfortable on the job,* Maxine thought. Yandy had on a pair of ripped-up blue jeans that hugged her hips, a tight T-shirt, and a pair of neon pink socks and flip flops.

"How are you, Yandy?" Maxine asked, just trying to have a friendly conversation.

"I'm doing fine. All I had to do today was encourage Pearl to walk the treadmill. I spent the rest of the day sitting on my ass doing absolutely nothing. By the way, you don't have to wear pants suits when you work here. Pearl lets us wear whatever we want. Prescott, Pearl's husband, will be coming home today. He's a nice old man that has a liking for us black women. I'm going to leave since you're familiar with what to do for Pearl. Today is awards day at my daughter's school and I don't want to be late," Yandy said then turned to Mrs. Deere.

"Momma, I'm getting ready to leave. Maxine's here!"

Mrs. Deere was looking out the bedroom window at the swans in the lake when Maxine walked into the bedroom to greet her.

"How are you doing, Pearl? It's a beautiful day outside. Would you like to get dressed and go sit on the patio?"

"Oh hello, Maxine. I'm so glad to see you. My energy level is low. I don't feel like doing anything, but you can help me shower. Yandy asked me earlier if I wanted to wash up, but I didn't feel up to it."

Maxine went to get some fresh linens for Mrs. Deere's bed. She noticed the sheets hadn't been changed since her last visit a week ago. Then she got the water warm for Mrs. Deere to take a shower.

"If you're ready to take your shower I'm ready to assist you, ma'am" Maxine said, trying to motivate Mrs. Deere.

"I'm ready. I move a little slow nowadays," Mrs. Deere said as she got out of the chair.

Maxine stood beside Mrs. Deere as she walked holding her hand to make sure she did not lose her balance.

"Would you like for me to step out while you get in the shower, Mrs. Deere?"

"Maxine, there's no need to step out of the bathroom. We have the same body parts. The only difference is mine are wrinkled and sagging, and yours are still tight and right," Mrs. Deere said laughing.

Maxine laughed so hard she felt as if she was going to pee on herself after hearing Mrs. Deere crack a joke. It was comforting to Mrs. Deere to have a caregiver to seem to care for her. As Maxine scrubbed her back with the soapy sponge, Mrs. Deere was thinking about the little things people take for granted until they get old and can't do them anymore. Once Mrs.

Deere dried herself off, she allowed Maxine to help her put her clothes on for the day.

"I feel so much better after that shower. Thank you for your motivation and assisting me. Let's go out and sit on the patio. What type of food do you like to eat, Maxine?"

"Italian food is my favorite, Ms. Pearl,"

"Press the intercom button and tell the chef to prepare some eggplant with pasta and meatballs," Mrs. Deere said while grabbing her walker.

Maxine and Mrs. Deere sat on the patio and watched the swans in the water while waiting for the chef to prepare dinner. The Italian food that the chef prepared was delicious.

"PEARL, LOVE.....," Prescott yelled as he walked into the estate.

"Mrs. Deere is outside with one of the caregivers," one of the housekeepers said as she dusted the furniture.

Mr. Deere walked to the kitchen window and saw his wife and the beautiful black woman sitting beside her. Prescott loved Pearl with all his heart, but there was something that he loved about a black woman. Mrs. Deere had had two hip replacements and was a manic depressive. After the many surgeries and taking all sorts of medication, her appearance had changed. Pearl had gained weight and didn't feel attractive to her husband anymore. Fearing that Mrs. Deere was going to try to commit suicide, Prescott hired someone to be with his wife for companionship 24 hours a day.

Prescott walked outside and passionately kissed his wife, happy to see that she was dress in clothes instead of her usual nightgown.

"Honey, it's so good to see you sitting outside enjoying the sun. And who do we have here?" he asked as he eyed Maxine up and down.

I know this old fart ain't giving me the motherfucking eye, Maxine thought as she gave a friendly smile.

"Prescott, honey, this is Maxine Gamble. She works for the nursing agency that you called to help Yandy and Holly out. I would love for you to make Maxine an offer that she can't refuse to keep me company around the house, lovebug," Mrs. Deere said, giving her husband the puppy dog look.

Mr. Deere focused his attention back to Maxine after his wife spoke.

"It's a pleasure to meet you, Maxine. My wife seems to have a great liking for you," he said with a look of lust in his eyes.

"It's a pleasure to meet you as well, sir. I can leave you two alone so that you can have some privacy."

Maxine wanted to go inside because Mr. Deere was still giving her the 'I Want to Just Fuck You' look, and Mrs. Deere wasn't picking up on the disrespectful vibe. "There's no need to leave us alone, Maxine. Let me join you two beautiful ladies so that we can discuss business," Mr. Deere said, sitting down at the table.

What A Deal

Maxine was so excited to talk to Charmaine about working for Mrs. Deere. Charmaine was happy to hear that Maxine was taking the job. Charmaine knew she would have gladly walked away from her position if the Deere family was looking for a registered nurse.

Later that day, Eva told Maxine that she was stopping over after work just to visit. Maxine was in the kitchen preparing dinner when Eva arrived.

"What up, sis?" Eva said as she walked into the kitchen.

"Just cooking dinner, that's all," Maxine said, as she went into the cabinet to get some garlic salt for the turkey.

"You're cooking a feast. Turkey, cornbread dressing, salad, green beans, candied yams and macaroni and cheese. What's up? You cooking for an army? Are you pregnant? Did the doctor propose to you, Maxine?"

Maxine put the macaroni and cheese in the oven. "I have a new job, Eva. When I say I'm grateful, girl, I'm grateful," Maxine said about to cry, thinking about how good God is.

"Where are you going to be working now, Ms. Moving Up the Ladder?" Eva asked, feeling a bit jealous.

"I'm going to be working private duty as a caregiver for this well-to-do family that really likes me."

"Maxine, you're going backwards. You mean to tell me that you're going to quit a job that gives you weekends and holidays off to take a job wiping ass and serving food for a client who might die the next day and leave you without a job?" Eva asked with her hand on her hip.

"Yeah, Eva that's exactly what I'm going to do. I'm getting paid twenty-five dollars per hour with insurance that will cover vision and dental for my family starting the first day of work. Oh, and I will be getting paid every week. I would wipe your ass if you paid me that per hour. Plus, the lady's husband gave me a welcome bonus of $2,000," Maxine responded, pulling the check out of her purse to show it to her sister.

"Are they looking for a part-time ass wiper?" Eva joked.

When Eva looked at the name on the check, her eyes widened.

"You're going to be working for the Deere family as in Deere Noosa's company?" she asked.

Maxine laughed so hard that she peed on herself a little bit.

"Yes, the one and only girl. Hallelujah."

First Official Day at Work

Yandy and Holly weren't pleased to find out they would no longer be able to work any day they felt like working, after receiving the bad news that Maxine was going to be their permanent co-worker.

"I'm not happy that Pearl asked this Maxine chick to work for her. We must put together a plan to get her fired," Yandy said, mad as hell.

"I'm with whatever plan you come up with, because this bitch is intruding and taking our hours," Holly retorted as she walked around in the kitchen worried about someone coming into their work territory.

"Don't stress about the small stuff. I'm going to take care of our problem. Ain't nobody going to come in here and take our money if I got anything to do with it. Maxine is parking her car right now. Pretend to be delighted that she's going to be working with us. Put on the bullshit happy face. Here she comes," Yandy muttered as she smiled, giving her mother the evil eye to do as she said.

Yandy and Holly were both at the Deere's estate that day because it was payday. Mrs. Deere wanted her private duty caregivers to welcome Maxine as their new co-worker. Maxine walked into the estate in a navy blue, linen pants suit looking like she was arriving for a board meeting.

"Hello ladies," Maxine said as she walked in the room.

Both Yandy and Holly looked at Maxine with thoughts about getting rid of her quick. They noticed she was silently changing the dress code before their very eyes. The ladies walked into the den where Mrs. Deere was relaxing. Mrs. Deere had already told Yandy that she hired Maxine, so she knew what the meeting was all about.

"Holly and Yandy, I would like for you to welcome Maxine to the group. From now on you all will work in rotation so that everyone has some time off to spend with their family. Yandy and Holly, I know that you two liked being the only ones working here permanently, but I asked only the best to join you," Mrs. Deere said to get reaction from Holly and Yandy but got nothing negative in return.

"It's nice to have you working with us, Maxine. We are getting ready to get out of here and go shopping," Yandy said as she reached for her check from Mrs. Deere.

Holly grabbed her check from Mrs. Deere with a fake smile and said, "Thank you and welcome to the team!"

Maxine knew that Holly and Yandy weren't happy about her working with them permanently, but she didn't care. She could read their negative facial expressions a mile away. After the witches left, Maxine started tending to Mrs. Deere's needs. She went into the kitchen, poured a tall glass of tea, and grabbed a napkin. That's when she saw a few utility bills. The gas bill was $77.61. The water bill was $50, and the sewer bill was $134.67. Maxine couldn't understand why the poor people paid out the ass for utilities and the rich stayed rich by not paying hardly anything to keep warm and wash their butts. *Yandy and her mother must have been going through the Deere's mail that's why it's in here in the kitchen on the counter,* Maxine thought. She walked back into the den with the glass of tea and napkin in hand and placed it beside Mrs. Deere on the table.

"Thank you, Maxine. I knew I was getting the best when I got you," Mrs. Deere said with a grin.

Seven Months

It had been seven months, and Holly and Yandy
weren't successful with getting rid of Maxine. They
would not complete certain duties, thinking that
Maxine would confront them about it. But that never
happened. What they didn't know was Maxine's work
background. Maxine could do all the house staff
duties and take care of Mrs. Deere seven days a week
if she had to. Working those crazy hours in the
hospital and dealing with some nurses that didn't
want to work prepared Maxine for working with
people like Yandy and Holly. Maxine thought it was
rather funny that they even thought she was
unaware of their plans to get her fired or make her
quit. Mrs. Deere hired Ruth, another caregiver, as a
favor to a good friend because the lady was in
desperate need of a job. Ruth was 48 years old and
very naive. If someone were to ask Ruth to jump, she
wouldn't ask how high; she would just start jumping.
Ruth would ask stupid questions about whether
Yandy and Holly liked her, but Maxine wouldn't
answer the question when asked. Drama was
something Maxine steered cleared of. She was there
to make money not so-called friends.

"Maxine, I know you told me you don't do bullshit; but should I confront Yandy to ask her why she sold me some of her food stamps when there wasn't anything on her EBT card?"

Maxine had to think *Really Ruth?* before she spoke. "How much did you buy from her?" Maxine asked curiously.

"I gave Yandy $180 cash for $260 in food stamps. You talk about embarrassed when I went shopping and had to unload all those groceries on the conveyor belt and leave them at the store. Yandy needs to give me my money back. I have been calling Yandy but she has been ignoring my calls."

Yandy is so damn greedy. How can she be making all this money and receive government assistance? Maxine thought as she looked at the EBT card with Yandy's name on it.

"Do whatever you feel you should do, Ruth. Just don't buy her food stamps again. Are you working tomorrow?"

"Yeah, I'm working tomorrow unfortunately."

"Well, see you tomorrow. Have a good evening," Maxine said as she walked out of the front door after giving a verbal report.

Dinner and Dancing

Chad was happy to know that Maxine was coming over for dinner. They both had been working long hours and hadn't had time for one another. Maxine still hadn't introduced Chad to her sons. *It's been over a year, and I wonder why Maxine still hasn't introduce me to her sons. Is it because I haven't put a ring on her finger? Is she still being cautious?* Chad thought as he lit a few candles to set the mood. When the doorbell rang, Chad rushed to the door.

"Hey beautiful," he said, looking down at Maxine who was dressed in a black linen pants suit.

Before arriving, Maxine had taken off the white button-down shirt under the suit jacket. She wanted to show some cleavage to give some extra sex appeal. Maxine reached up to give Chad a passionate kiss.

"Hey handsome! What's smelling so good in here? I starved myself today just because you said you were cooking dinner for me," she said as she put her purse and key down on the table.

"It's a surprise. Slip into something a little more comfortable and come get your glass of wine while I finish setting the table."

Maxine gave Chad another kiss before going to take a quick shower. After getting her body relaxed and cleaned, she put on a red lace slip dress and satin black robe with a pair of clear, five-inch heel slipper shoes that had black feathers on them. Maxine felt sexy and looked forward to a romantic evening dancing by the fireplace with Chad. She walked into the kitchen and took a seat at the table. Chad handed her a glass of wine.

"Are you sure you're hungry because we can be doing something else while you watch me eat?" Chad said as he winked at her.

"I'm hungry, Chad. If you don't fix me something to eat it's going to be a fight up in here tonight, baby boy!"

Chad laughed at Maxine trying to be mean to him while he fixed her plate of food. He had cooked shrimp scampi and garlic bread with a side salad. They ate dinner together had great conversation then went to the bedroom to watch television. Maxine laid in Chad's strong arms as she rubbed his chest gently until he fell sleep. *It's not about having sex when we're together all of time, but I sure could have gone for a rodeo ride tonight,* Maxine thought as she held Chad's penis in her hand. She drifted off to sleep not having enough energy to be the aggressor.

Bold

Tension had been in the air between Maxine and the mother/daughter duo at work. One morning, Yandy texted Maxine by mistake before she had gotten out of bed. *Hey Ruth! Hope that you had a great weekend. Thanks for switching shifts with me so that I wouldn't cross paths with that bitch Maxine. Pearl and Prescott were wondering if you could pick up some whole wheat bagels, cream cheese and Lox's before coming to work.* ☺ *See ya,* it read. Maxine moved Chad's arm from around her waist and sat up so that she could call Ruth. She had a lengthy conversation with Ruth about the text message.

Ruth agreed to call Yandy and tell her that she was still coming in for work at 9 a.m. as promised. Yandy didn't realize that she sent the text message to the wrong person, because she was up to no good as usual. Maxine arrived at 8:30 a.m. to work in Ruth's place and to confront Yandy about the text message sent to her by mistake. Following Ruth's routine, Maxine drove around to the back of the Deere's estate to park her car. The garage door was up as Ruth told her it would be, and Yandy's car was running like normal. Maxine walked from the garage into the kitchen wondering if Yandy would be waiting there, but she wasn't.

Maxine walked down the hallway and peeped inside of Mr. Deere's office. She couldn't believe her eyes. Yandy was fucking some random dude in the Deere home like she owned the damn estate. Ruth's stories about Yandy were true. *This bitch is crazy, and has lost her motherfucking mind,* Maxine thought as she stared at her co-worker fucking. The stranger eased Yandy's lower half up and down slowly, watching her booty bounce when it came back down on his manhood.

"Work that shit, Yandy," the random dude said in a gangster tone, biting his bottom lip and pumping her slowly.

Feeling like someone was watching, Yandy looked over her shoulder and was surprised to see Maxine standing there. She quickly eased up off the random dude and put on her pants as her male friend did the same.

"What are you doing here, Maxine?" Yandy asked, shocked to see her.

"Does it matter why I'm here to work? Who is this person in Mr. and Mrs. Deere's house? You better be glad none of the maids caught you fucking in Mr. Deere's office," Maxine said with an attitude. Luckily, Mr. Deere had given the house staff a day off. Yandy ignored the questions and told her male friend to get in the car. Maxine followed behind Yandy to get an answer, daring her to disrespect her.

It was 8:50 a.m. and Maxine heard footsteps coming down the stairs into the kitchen. Innocent eyes looked at Maxine as though they saw a ghost. The children didn't recognize Maxine.

"Good morning," the kids said showing that they had been taught some manners from Ruth.

Ruth had to teach Yandy's children that it wasn't respectful to see someone and not to acknowledge them.

"Good morning, babies," Maxine said as she looked at Yandy's kids then their mother.

"Yandy, you and your momma are something else if no one has ever let it be known. Your trifling ass is up in your employer's estate fucking some random dude in your boss office. Not to mention your babies coming from the second floor with their overnight bags. They've been here the whole weekend, haven't they? Being too damn comfortable is a bad thing, and the shit is going to catch up with your thieving ass." Maxine said, releasing all the things that she had built up inside.

"Fuck you, Maxine," Yandy said with anger as she walked towards the door leading to the garage.

"No fuck you, bitch, and next time you send a text message make sure you're sending it to the right person. Mr. and Mrs. Deere pay us a decent wage to take care of our families, and then you and your momma bring that ghetto shit out here so the people can talk about our asses – when they catch you and *yo* momma fucking up," Maxine said, ready to 'fight a bitch'.

Yandy gave Maxine a dirty look before leaving. Maxine wasn't shaking in her boots when she caught the stare from Yandy. She was so ready to kick her ass.

Date

Eva drove with a smile on her face as she thought about her special friend. It was a blessing that Tyson wanted to spend the night at Maxine's house. *I wonder what our date is going to be like tonight,* Eva thought as she pulled up and saw Bobby sitting on the porch waiting for her.

"Bruh, give me some skin. She is pretty and got a nice ass ride, dawg. You better keep her, especially if she's holding down a full-time job," Bobby's brother, Ace, said staring at Eva from the porch.

"Man please, I've had many women with jobs since I moved here to Saint Louis. This one here: I'm just feeling for the moment. If she allows me to move in with her then I will claim her as my woman, but until then she's just in the lady friend category," Bobby replied as he walked down the steps.

Eva couldn't stop blushing as Bobby got closer to the car. She looked at him from head to toe. Dressed in a pair of blue jeans and a polo shirt with a clean-shaven face and the smell of cologne, Bobby knew how to turn the women on.

"Hey beautiful, you're looking good. How was your day at work?"

"Well thank you for the compliment, Bobby. You're not looking bad yourself. My day was all work. I didn't even get a lunch break. So, we're going out for dinner tonight instead of the movies, right?"

"Wherever you want to go, beautiful, is alright with me. Maybe later you'll let me rub your feet and relax your mind."

Eva grinned from ear to ear. There was something about Bobby that turned Eva on. Intuition was telling Eva she should leave this loser of a man alone. Bobby was a 51-year-old construction worker who moved from the south to work and live with his brother while down on his luck. He hoped to get back on his feet financially soon.

"Bobby, we're going to go to this bar and grill not too far from your brother's house."

"I'm a passenger; take me wherever you want to go."

Eva continued to smile and drive. Bobby leaned over to expose one of Eva's breasts and began licking and sucking her nipple.

"Bobby, stop; I'm going to lose control of my car and run into something."

"That's what I want you to do, Eva. Lose control with me. *Fo'get* about going to the bar and grill. Let's go to your place and order some food and chill out there!"

"You know I told you that I'm not ready to show you where I live, Bobby. If you want to get a hotel room, then we can do that instead and order a pizza or something."

"Lead the way, beautiful," Bobby said as his eyes opened then closed.

Within five minutes, Bobby nodded off to sleep as Eva drove to a hotel. *I should know better than to be messing around with a low life ass nigga, but I like him a lot. He's humorous, attentive and a freak,* Eva thought as she watched him snore. She pulled into the parking lot of a three-star hotel, parked her car, and then leaned over to wake Bobby with a kiss. Bobby was snoring like a bear. Eva had to nudge him to wake him up from his deep sleep.

"Ok sexy, let's do this," he said.

Eva and Bobby walked in the hotel holding hands like a married couple.

"I'm going to use the restroom while you pay for the room, Bobby."

Eva gave Bobby a passionate kiss before walking away. *Damn, I thought Eva was going to pay for the room since she doesn't want me to know where the fuck she lives,* Bobby thought.

Eva walked out of the restroom with a smile on her face, thinking of Bobby rubbing her feet and other parts of her body.

"Sir, your credit card declined," the desk clerk said respectfully.

Bobby turned to Eva.

"Beautiful, give the lady your credit card and I'll give you the money for the cost of the hotel room," he requested.

Say what. Motherfucker? It's bad enough yo broke ass don't have a car to come pick me up or your own place where I can serve you my ass on possibly clean sheets. Now you're asking me to hand over my credit card to cover the hotel room? Eva thought.

"Bobby, let's go. I'm not handing over my credit card to pay for the hotel room. I don't care how much money you have in your pocket, buddy."

"Beautiful, don't be like that."

Eva walked out of the hotel and headed towards her car. She was embarrassed about being with a man with bad credit and was ready to drop his ass off. She drove 90 miles per hour and didn't say a word until she pulled up in front of Bobby's brother's house.

"Bobby, I can't continue to see you anymore. You're too old to be in these types of life situations. For one night, I wanted you to remember everything you did with me yet I can smell alcohol on your breath. You can't afford a hotel room to even get laid without asking for a woman's financial assistance."

Bobby listened to Eva bitch at him.

"Are you finished talking?" he asked while keeping his composure.

Eva gave approval for Bobby to talk but wanted him to get out of her car after having his say. She never wanted to see his black ass again.

"It's not like I didn't have the money to pay for the hotel room, beautiful. I just forgot to pay my credit card bill; you dig. I asked you to just put the charges on your credit card, and you chose not to do it. You were the one that fucked up the date tonight. It wasn't because of the alcohol you could smell on my breath. Give me some suga, and stop being so mad all the damn time, Eva" he said.

Eva gave Bobby a kiss which led to them to talking in her car until they fell asleep.

When Eva opened her eyes, the sun was coming up. *Unbelievable! No one would ever believe that I have a fully furnished home but skipped dinner and slept in my car with a man in his brother's driveway all night,* Eva thought while watching Bobby snore.

"Bobby, wake up! I need to use the bathroom somewhere and go home to shower before going to work!" she exclaimed, feeling like a fool.

Bobby looked over at Eva as he rubbed his eyes trying to wake up.

"Good morning, beautiful. I hate to see you go, but I know you must go to work. Do you mind coming back over tonight and maybe we can have dinner together?" he asked.

Eva agreed to come back over after work while rushing Bobby out of her car. She really had to use the bathroom. Bobby got out of the car and walked to his brother's front door, pressing the doorbell. It was 6:35 a.m. *I'm never going to see this asshole again. He doesn't even have a key to his brother's house to get in. What a shame,* Eva thought as she sat in her car till Bobby got in the house.

Be My Guest

Mrs. Deere asked Maxine to accompany her to lunch to visit a dear friend, Marci Ko. Marci Ko was in the fur business and celebrating her retirement after turning the family business over to her daughters. Before waving Pearl in her direction, Marci turned the 15-carat diamond ring to the palm of her hand so that only the band would show.

"Pearl, I'm over here darling," Marci said excited to see her longtime friend.

Mrs. Deere smiled when she saw Marci Ko sitting at the table with drinks waiting like old times. Maxine read Marci's fake smile as she and Mrs. Deere got closer to the table.

"What time would you like for me to come back and pick you up, Pearl?" Maxine asked as she helped her sit down in the chair at the table.

Maxine planned to go to one of the gift shops nearby to pass the time.

"You don't have to come back and pick me up. Please stay and be our guest," Mrs. Deere replied.

Maxine assumed that she was dropping off Mrs. Deere to eat lunch with her friend, especially seeing that she was the only black person in the restaurant.

Everyone was looking at her as though she were an alien.

"Ok, Mrs. Deere, let me go and wash my hands. I'll be right back," Maxine said. She really went to prepare herself for Marci Ko who had her nose all turned up.

Marci leaned over as though she was whispering to talk to Mrs. Deere but spoke loud enough for the people at the next table to hear. "Pearl, you didn't tell me that this Maxine woman you're so fond of is a Negro. I assumed she was some tall, pretty, blonde-haired college student when you said she was having lunch with us." Marci said then took a sip of tea.

"Marci, you shouldn't talk that way. Now you know I wouldn't put your life in danger as you claim occurs when you're around African Americans. Maxine is very intelligent. Look at the way she's dressed. She has class. Let's enjoy our lunch, shall we?" Mrs. Deere said, sipping her mimosa.

Maxine returned to the table with a friendly smile before acknowledging Marci formally.

"May I take your order, ladies?" the waiter asked with a stern look on his face.

Marci ordered an egg salad sandwich with a bowl of onion soup. Mrs. Deere ordered a turkey club sandwich on rye with a bowl of lobster bisque. Maxine claimed she was on a diet to avoid ordering lunch. She didn't like the way the young white waiter frowned at her when asking to take her order.

"So, Maxine, how long have you been doing this type of work?" Marci asked with intent to be nosey.

Maxine hoped Mrs. Deere would intervene and stop her friend from talking, but she didn't.

"I've been doing this type of work for a long time," Maxine replied, looking Marci dead in her eyes.

Marci took Maxine's look as a sign of disrespect since her grandparents owned slaves that took care of her hand and foot. She knew what wasn't tolerated.

"Pearl, isn't it strange when blacks come up with the strangest name for their children like Juwanna? Half of the time the children can't pronounce their names; and you better not ask them to spell the name," Marci said as she laughed and glared right at Maxine.

Maxine couldn't believe the nerve of this old bitch trying to test her patience.

"Marci, is that your correct name? You need to put a little more grip cream to keep your dentures in place before saying another word, ma'am. It's so unattractive to see your gums when you're talking. Pearl, I'll be back when I think you're ready to go," Maxine said as she got up from the table to leave.

Once Maxine left, Mrs. Deere spoke.

"Marci, now you have pissed off my favorite caregiver! I told you Maxine was a smart one. She caught on to your rudeness right away," Mrs. Deere said, laughing at Maxine's joke about the dentures.

Maxine was relieved to be back at the Deere's estate after her experience with Marci Ko. She didn't care if she never saw that old Hag ever again. Before leaving the Deere home, Maxine wrote the day's activities in the logbook. Holly and Maxine never saw eye to eye, so they had to read each other's notes to communicate with one another. As soon as Maxine heard Holly walking into the house from the garage, she walked out of the front door. Holly put away her coat and fixed a milkshake for Mr. Deere. Then she read Maxine's notes and instantly got jealous. It burned her up that Maxine left the house with Mrs. Deere.

Holly always hoped to be a good enough caregiver to end up in a client's will. She felt she was due something for her good service. Yandy wasn't thinking on that level. She just wanted to immediately spend every penny she got and not think about her future. As private duty workers, the mother daughter duo knew they'd have to start all over and find a new family to work for when their client died. That's why Yandy and Holly wanted to get to know some of Mr. and Mrs. Deere's friends personally — to make sure they had a good list of potential clients.

Pearl is taking Maxine around all her rich friends. I'm going to start dressing just like Maxine in my two-piece suits, and then maybe Pearl will want to hang out with her friends on the days I work. I need to mingle with them, Holly thought after closing the logbook.

The next morning, Yandy came in wearing a pair of black tights, a light blue low cut Ralph Lauren T-shirt, and a pair of black, high top Converse sneakers. She was carrying a 40-ounce beer wrapped in a brown paper bag when she greeted her mother. "What's up? How are Pearl's and Prescott's old asses doing today?" Yandy said, plopping down on the plush living room chair.

"Pearl and Prescott are doing alright; they're resting in the bedroom. You aren't going to believe this shit that I'm getting ready to tell you. Guess who Pearl took that bitch, Maxine, around yesterday for lunch?"

"Who? I'm not into the guessing game."

"Marci Ko. I just can't believe Pearl took Maxine around anybody that she knows, and we haven't met anyone that she's friends with."

"I feel you on that note. We have been working for Pearl for too damn long to not have met at least one of her well-to-do friends."

"Yes, you're right. To get a chance to rub shoulders with Mrs. Ko; and this bitch, Maxine, got lucky enough to be around her all day! I wonder what they talked about. From now on, I know what I'm going to do," Holly said, pacing the floor.

"What is the plan?" Yandy asked, feeling a buzz from the beer she drank before she arrived at work.

"I'm going to start dressing just like Maxine," Holly replied.

Yandy was annoyed.

"For what? Keep being you. Don't turn into someone else, Maxine is kissing ass to be in our position. Pearl and Prescott love us. We ain't going nowhere. You're stressing for nothing. I'm going to put my beer in the refrigerator," Yandy said, unbothered about the job situation.

After talking to Maxine, Ruth was a little wiser at work. She needed to keep her job. She had four teenagers to feed and had recently broken up with her boyfriend who had helped pay the bills. As routine, Yandy had the garage door up and her car running so that she could be ready to go once Ruth arrived. Ruth had to toot her horn several times to let Yandy know that she had arrived so that she could move her car. When Yandy didn't open the garage door, Ruth got impatient. After Ruth got her on the phone, Yandy yelled for her children to get in the car.

Ruth focused her attention off her phone and back on the garage. That's when she saw little feet running by getting in the car as the garage door went up. *Yandy is still sneaking and bringing her kids to work,* Ruth thought. She could not understand why Prescott, Pearl or even the housekeeping staff hadn't caught Yandy bringing her kids to work. As Yandy backed out of the garage, Ruth drove in her place waving bye to the children sitting in Yandy's back seat. *You can't get away with doing bad things forever,* Ruth thought as she got out of her car shaking her head.

Rejuvenated

Maxine was happy to return to work after being off for four days. She was already prepared to take Mrs. Deere to the therapist at 9 a.m., to her regular Thursday beauty shop appointment at 2, and then to lunch at the Frontenac Cafe. When Maxine arrived to work at 7 a.m., Ruth was there to greet her with a friendly smile. She filled Maxine in on what went on during her days off. Mr. Deere had a terrible fall and was on bed rest until his body healed properly. Mrs. Deere had cancelled all her appointments for the day.

"It looks like you're going to have an easy workday, Maxine. I hope you have some good reading material," Ruth said smiling.

"I do have a couple of books in my bag: one is titled 'C That's Why I Don't Fool with Women' laugh out loud by Sherre Still," Maxine chuckled as she told Ruth about the book. "I have another book by the same author called 'Non-Disclosure'. I hate to hear that Mr. Deere had a fall. Did he hit his head?"

"No, and that's what kept him from being admitted into the hospital. Yandy had taken him to one of those antique shops in Clayton to sell some rare coins he got when he was in the war. He lost his balance while Yandy was on her cell phone standing right beside him," Ruth said in a low tone, not wanting the housekeeper to hear their conversation.

"I can't understand why Yandy and Holly are still working for the Deeres. The Deere children need to be aware that those two are a fucking health risk to their parents," Maxine said as she shook her head.

This was now a personal issue to Maxine because she felt like an advocate for the Deeres. *I'm going to call the Deere children and ask them to fly-in for a visit with their parents. This way they can see the problem for themselves,* Maxine thought. The Deeres' children hadn't seen their parents in years. They were raised by nannies most of their lives and really didn't know their parents.

"I hear you, Maxine. I hope their day comes real soon. Yandy is still bringing her kids to work too," Ruth added as she grabbed her purse and car keys off the kitchen table.

Maxine just shook her head. This situation was just mind blowing. Ruth waved bye before walking out the door. She was headed to get some rest before having to report back at 11 p.m. to relieve Maxine.

Maxine went to Mr. and Mrs. Deere's bedroom to greet them then went to ask the chef to prepare them some breakfast. Mr. Deere thanked Maxine for helping take care of him even though she was only there to take care of his wife. Maxine noticed a slight change in Mrs. Deere. She wasn't as friendly towards her.

Mrs. Deere ate breakfast in silence and got dressed on her own without Maxine's assistance. Pearl had written a to do list unbeknownst to her caregiver, instead of speaking directly to her – and had sent home the housekeeping staff. Of course, the staff was happy to be sent home with pay for the day. From the time the staff left the estate, Maxine had washed two loads of laundry, cleaned the master bedroom, dusted all the furniture, emptied the trash, and vacuumed the carpet throughout the estate. She hadn't worked that hard cleaning her own house. Finally, Maxine was able to take a break. She joined Mrs. Deere on the front porch.

"Maxine, would you mind raking the leaves and taking care of the backyard before you leave for the day, please? That's if you don't mind," Mrs. Deere said as she brushed her fingers through her hair.

Maxine felt the vibe that Mrs. Deere had an issue with her.

"Pearl, I do mind raking your lawn. You have a grounds person to take care of that. Why assign me to do so?"

"If I were you, I would do anything to put food on the table and provide for your family, especially being a single parent, sweetheart," Mrs. Deere quickly replied, trying to belittle her help.

I know I didn't hear this old hag correctly, Maxine thought. Mrs. Deere had this sinister look on her face as though she was ready to slap Maxine if she said another word back to her. *How dare this nigger refuse to do something that I ask her to do? I've been good to her. Never will she work among my circle of friends or do private duty work for anyone else, and I will see to that,* Mrs. Deere thought, still looking at Maxine sideways.

Maxine never felt comfortable calling Mrs. Deere by her first name until that day, because she was being disrespected.

"Well Pearl, I hope this doesn't seem disrespectful but you're not me. And if raking your leaves is what I must do here to put food on the table for my family then today is my last day," Maxine said with an attitude.

Mrs. Deere squinted her eyes and looked directly at Maxine like a Siamese cat getting ready to scratch. Pearl had never in her entire life had the "help" get smart with her.

"Maxine, you're not ever going to do this line of work again. I made you relevant with my circle of friends. You were hired to take care of me until I die. If you think you're going to work for Marci Ko, I will never allow that to be," she said.

Maxine was trying to figure out where Pearl got the crazy idea that she would ever want to work for that bitch, Marci Ko. She decided that would be her last day because Pearl spoke as if she owned her. Furthermore, she didn't care how much money Mr. Deere was paying her. It wasn't worth losing her pride.

"Pearl, thank you for the opportunity to work with you. I will ask Prescott to give me my check before I leave," Maxine said as she got up from the lawn chair to leave the front porch.

Maxine told Prescott about the disagreement with his wife. Mr. Deere wrote Maxine a check, shook her hand and wished her well. Maxine gathered her personal belongings, got in her car, drove away, and didn't look back. *What a shame that Pearl thinks she can keep me from making money to provide for my family if I don't work for her. Hell, I just got hired with a nursing agency to work tomorrow morning,* Maxine thought as she closed the app on her cell phone after applying for the job.

No One Has Ever

Mrs. Deere was back in a deep depression, and everyone knew it was because Maxine had quit. Mr. Deere was willing to offer Maxine more money to return. He knew she was the reason for his wife's sadness; but Mrs. Deere wouldn't allow her husband to contact Maxine. It had been a year since Maxine had resigned, and it was apparent his wife missed the long conversations and quality time that they spent together. She never enjoyed living in her home nor did she really appreciate having someone to care for her until Maxine came into her life.

Pearl and Prescott worked long hours six days a week running their family business and never took much time to enjoy life. When the Deeres' four children were small, they hired two nannies to take care of all their needs until they shipped them all off to boarding school. When the children grew up and got married, they never visited their parents because they didn't know them that well. Every now and then, their children would call to find out if their parents were still alive. They were really checking on their inheritance.

While working for the Deeres, Maxine shared that her parents too worked long hours running their church and deprived themselves of what was important:

family. Mrs. Deere thought of Maxine as a surrogate daughter and that's why she took her around her friends, because she trusted and loved Maxine.

After Yandy told Mrs. Deere that Marci Ko called asking for Maxine's contact info, Mrs. Deere felt betrayed. Yandy's lie was elaborate, even mentioning that Marci needed to find out which hours would work best for Maxine since she had accepted the job. Every day since Maxine left, Mrs. Deere thought Maxine had been working for Marci. She thought this even though Marci promised her she would never approach Mrs. Deere's help for herself. When Mrs. Deere gave in and talked to Marci, she reassured her friend that Maxine wasn't working for her.

"We are friends, Pearl, I can't believe that's why you haven't been talking to me. There would be no way I would have colored people in my home working for me. They're not to be trusted, and they learn things too fast. I don't want 'em to end up trying to be an entrepreneur like me," Marci explained as she told her Spanish maid to shut the door so that her conversation wouldn't be overheard.

After Mrs. Deere got off the phone with her friend, she called for Yandy. Mrs. Deere was home alone and didn't know her caregiver wasn't in the house. The second time Mrs. Deere called out for Yandy, she got so upset at being ignored that it impacted her breathing and blood pressure. Her heart failed as she experienced a stroke, and Mrs. Deere breathed her last breath, dying suddenly.

Yandy left the estate to go to another private duty assignment she and Holly had finally acquired. The mother and daughter duo felt that soon Pearl and Prescott would be meeting their maker, so they began working for someone else. Still in her comfort zone at work, Yandy left Mrs. Deere alone when she thought she was asleep. She went to take care of her new client with intent to come right back. *My pockets are going to be fat when I get paid on Friday,* Yandy thought while helping the new client get in bed after changing the man's disposable underwear and bed linens.

It Finally Caught Up with Them

Maxine was back in school because Chad had encouraged her to enroll now "not later". While studying for an exam, Maxine sipped some hot tea. Her phone ringing incessantly broke her train of thought. It was Ruth.

"Hi Ruth! Are things still going okay for you at the Deeres?" Maxine asked, happy to hear from her former coworker.

"Girl, Pearl died Tuesday while Prescott was out of town on his deer hunting trip. Yandy was scheduled to work the 7 p.m. to 7 a.m. shift. The neighbors said they saw Yandy leave around 11:30 p.m. Remember when I told you about the two young white girls Mr. Deere hired to replace you about six months ago? One of the young ladies Sybil came in early for work, because she was having car trouble. She got dropped off at 5:30 a.m. I know the exact time because it's written in the logbook."

Ruth continued, after taking a breath. "Sybil called the paramedics after finding Pearl slumped over in bed unresponsive. The paramedics took Pearl to the hospital and pronounced her dead-on arrival. Sybil called Prescott and the rest of the family to tell them how she found Pearl when she arrived. One of the maids told me that Yandy had walked in the Deeres' house in shock. I believe she was initially working up a quick lie to tell Mrs. Deere until she noticed she wasn't there. The police came out today to ask Sybil more questions about the day Pearl died. Prescott is devastated over Pearl's death and wants us to be here for him. The Deere children will fly in once the memorial arrangement are made. Prescott said the police are going to charge Yandy for negligence, because she's a caregiver and wasn't in the home when Pearl had the stroke and died."

"Oh man!" Maxine paused. "I have to say I'm so glad I quit working for the Deeres when I did. I would have been guilty by association working with those low-life bitches. They didn't want to accept that there was enough money to be made for everyone. There was no reason to be so cutthroat and try to get someone fired."

Ruth and Maxine spoke for a little longer about the Deeres and what would come of everything. Ruth mentioned something about Mr. Deere wanting to apologize to Maxine. This peaked both of their curiosities but who really knew what it all meant.

Would Maxine and Mr. Deere get the chance to speak? Would Yandy and Holly's shortcomings get fully exposed? Would Ruth continue to work for Mr. Deere after his loss?

Only the "Chronicles" will tell. *Stay tuned for Part 2...*